CW00932934

IN THE MOU
BY
ELIZABETH VON
ARNIM

IN THE MOUNTAINS

July 22nd.

I want to be quiet now.

I crawled up here this morning from the valley like a sick ant,—struggled up to the little house on the mountain side that I haven't seen since the first August of the war, and dropped down on the grass outside it, too tired even to be able to thank God that I had got home.

Here I am once more, come back alone to the house that used to be so full of happy life that its little wooden sides nearly burst with the sound of it. I never could have dreamed that I would come back to it alone. Five years ago, how rich I was in love; now how poor, how stripped of all I had. Well, it doesn't matter. Nothing matters. I'm too tired. I want to be quiet now. Till I'm not so tired. If only I can be quiet....

July 23rd.

Yesterday all day long I lay on the grass in front of the door and watched the white clouds slowly passing one after the other at long, lazy intervals over the tops of the delphiniums,—the row of delphiniums I planted all those years ago. I didn't think of anything; I just lay there in the hot sun, blinking up and counting the intervals between one spike being reached and the next. I was conscious of the colour of the delphiniums, jabbing up stark into the sky, and of how blue they were; and yet not so blue, so deeply and radiantly blue, as the sky. Behind them was the great basin of space filled with that other blue of the air, that lovely blue with violet shades in it; for the mountain I am on drops sharply away from the edge of my tiny terrace-garden, and the whole of the space between it and the mountains opposite brims all day long with blue and violet light. At night the bottom of the valley looks like water, and the lamps in the little town lying along it like quivering reflections of the stars.

I wonder why I write about these things. As if I didn't know them! Why do I tell myself in writing what I already so well know? Don't I know about the mountain, and the brimming cup of blue light? It is because, I suppose, it's lonely to stay inside oneself. One has to come out and talk. And if there is no one to talk to one imagines someone, as though one were writing a letter to somebody who loves one, and who will want to know, with the sweet eagerness and solicitude of love, what one does and what the place one is in looks like. It makes one feel less lonely to think like this,—to write it down, as if to one's friend who cares. For I'm afraid of loneliness; shiveringly, terribly afraid. I don't mean the ordinary physical loneliness, for here I am, deliberately travelled away from London to get to it, to its spaciousness and healing. I mean that awful loneliness of spirit that is the ultimate tragedy of life. When you've got to that, really reached it, without hope, without escape, you die. You just can't bear it, and you die.

July 24th.

It's queer the urge one has to express oneself, to get one's self into words. If I weren't alone I wouldn't write, of course, I would talk. But nearly everything I wanted to say would be things I couldn't say. Not unless it was to some wonderful, perfect, all-understanding listener,—the sort one used to imagine God was in the days when one said prayers. Not quite like God though either, for this listener would sometimes say something kind and gentle, and sometimes, stroke one's hand a little to show that he understood. Physically, it is most blessed to be alone. After all that has happened, it is most blessed. Perhaps I shall grow well here, alone. Perhaps just sitting on these honey-scented grass slopes will gradually heal me. I'll sit and lick my wounds. I do so dreadfully want to get mended! I do so dreadfully want to get back to confidence in goodness.

July 25th.

For three days now I've done nothing but lie in the sun, except when meals are put in the open doorway for me. Then I get up reluctantly, like some sleepy animal, and go and eat them and come out again.

In the evening it is too cold and dewy here for the grass, so I drag a deep chair into the doorway and sit and stare at the darkening sky and the brightening stars. At ten o'clock Antoine, the man of all work who has looked after the house in its years of silence during the war, shuts up everything except this door and withdraws to his own room and his wife;

and presently I go in too, bolting the door behind me, though there is nothing really to shut out except the great night, and I creep upstairs and fall asleep the minute I'm in bed. Indeed, I don't think I'm much more awake in the day than in the night. I'm so tired that I want to sleep and sleep; for years and years; for ever and ever.

There was no unpacking to do. Everything was here as I left it five years ago. We only took, five years ago, what each could carry, waving goodbye to the house at the bend of the path and calling to it as the German soldiers called to their disappearing homes, 'Back for Christmas!' So that I came again to it with only what I could carry, and had nothing to unpack. All I had to do was to drop my little bag on the first chair I found and myself on to the grass, and in that position we both stayed till bedtime.

Antoine is surprised at nothing. He usedn't to be surprised at my gaiety, which yet might well have seemed to him, accustomed to the sobriety of the peasant women here, excessive; and nor is he now surprised at my silence. He has made a few inquiries as to the health and whereabouts of the other members of that confident group that waved goodbyes five years ago, and showed no surprise when the answer, at nearly every name, was 'Dead.' He has married since I went away, and hasn't a single one of the five children he might have had, and he doesn't seem surprised at that either. I am. I imagined the house, while I was away, getting steadily fuller, and used to think that when I came back I would find little Swiss babies scattered all over it; for, after all, there quite well might have been ten, supposing Antoine had happened to possess a natural facility in twins.

July 26th.

The silence here is astonishing. There are hardly any birds. There is hardly any wind, so that the leaves are very still and the grass scarcely stirs. The crickets are busy, and the sound of the bells on distant cows pasturing higher up on the mountains floats down to me; but else there is nothing but a great, sun-flooded silence.

When I left London it was raining. The Peace Day flags, still hanging along the streets, drooped heavy with wet in what might have been November air, it was so dank and gloomy. I was prepared to arrive here in one of the mountain mists that settle down on one sometimes for days,—vast wet stretches of grey stuff like some cold, sodden blanket, muffling one away from the mountains opposite, and the valley, and the sun. Instead I found summer: beautiful clear summer, fresh and warm together as only summer up on these honey-scented slopes can be, with the peasants beginning to cut the grass,—for things happen a month later here than down in the valley, and if you climb higher you can catch up June, and by climbing higher and higher you can climb, if you want to, right back into the spring. But you don't want to if you're me. You don't want to do anything but stay quiet where you are.

July 27th.

If only I don't think—if only I don't think and remember—how can I not get well again here in the beauty and the gentleness? There's all next month, and September, and perhaps October too may be warm and golden. After that I must go back, because the weather in this high place while it is changing from the calms of autumn to the calms of the exquisite alpine winter is a disagreeable, daunting thing. But I have two whole months; perhaps three. Surely I'll be stronger, tougher, by then? Surely I'll at least be better? I couldn't face the winter in London if this desperate darkness and distrust of life is still in my soul. I don't want to talk about my soul. I hate to. But what else am I to call the innermost *Me,* the thing that has had such wounds, that is so much hurt and has grown so dim that I'm in terror lest it should give up and go under, go quite out, and leave me alone in the dark?

July 28th.

It is dreadful to be so much like Job.

Like him I've been extraordinarily stripped of all that made life lovely. Like him I've lost, in a time that is very short to have been packed so full of disasters, nearly everything I loved. And it wasn't only the war. The war passed over me, as it did over everybody, like some awful cyclone, flattening out hope and fruitfulness, leaving blood and ruins behind it; but it wasn't only that. In the losses of the war, in the anguish of losing one's friends, there was the grisly comfort of companionship in grief; but beyond and besides that life has been devastated for me. I do feel like Job, and I can't bear it. It is so humiliating, being so much

2

stricken. I feel ridiculous as well as wretched; as if somebody had taken my face and rubbed it in dust.

And still, like Job, I cling on to what I can of trust in goodness, for if I let that go I know there would be nothing left but death.

July 29th.

Oh, what is all this talk of death? To-day I suddenly noticed that each day since I've been here what I've written down has been a whine, and that each day while I whined I was in fact being wrapped round by beautiful things, as safe and as perfectly cared for *really* as a baby fortunate enough to have been born into the right sort of family. Oughtn't I to be ashamed? Of course I ought; and so I am. For, looking at the hours, each hour as I get to it, they are all good. Why should I spoil them, the ones I'm at now, by the vivid remembrance, the aching misery, of those black ones behind me? They, anyhow, are done with; and the ones I have got to now are plainly good. And as for Job who so much haunted me yesterday, I can't really be completely like him, for at least I've not yet had to take a potsherd and sit down somewhere and scrape. But perhaps I had better touch wood over that, for one has to keep these days a wary eye on God.

Mrs. Antoine, small and twenty-five, who has been provided by Antoine, that expert in dodging inconveniences, with a churn suited to her size out of which she produces little pats of butter suited to my size every day, Switzerland not having any butter in it at all for sale,—Mrs. Antoine looked at me to-day when she brought out food at dinner time, and catching my eye she smiled at me; and so I smiled at her, and instantly she began to talk.

Up to now she has crept about softly on the tips of her toes as if she were afraid of waking me, and I had supposed it to be her usual fashion of moving and that it was natural to her to be silent; but to-day, after we had smiled at each other, she stood over me with a dish in one hand and a plate in the other, and held forth at length with the utmost blitheness, like some carolling blacks bird, about her sufferings, and the sufferings of Antoine, and the sufferings of everybody during the war. The worse the sufferings she described had been the blither became her carollings; and with a final chirrup of the most flute-like cheerfulness she finished this way:

'Ah, ma foi, oui—il y avait un temps où il a fallu se fier entièrement au bon Dieu. C'était affreux.'

July 30th.

It's true that the worst pain is the remembering one's happiness when one is no longer happy and perhaps it may be just as true that past miseries end by giving one some sort of satisfaction. Just their being over must dispose one to regard them complacently. Certainly I already I remember with a smile and a not unaffectionate shrug troubles that seemed very dreadful a few years back. But this—this misery that has got me now, isn't it too deep, doesn't it cut too ruthlessly at the very roots of my life ever to be something that I will smile at? It seems impossible that I ever should. I think the remembrance of this year will always come like a knife cutting through any little happiness I may manage to collect. You see, what has happened has taken away my faith in *goodness*,—I don't know who *you* are that I keep on wanting to tell things to, but I must talk and tell you. Yes; that is what it has done; and the hurt goes too far down to be healed. Yet I know time is a queer, wholesome thing. I've lived long enough to have found that out. It is very sanitary. It cleans up everything. It never fails to sterilise and purify. Quite possibly I shall end by being a wise old lady who discourses with, the utmost sprightliness, after her regular meals, on her past agonies, and extracts much agreeable entertainment from them, even is amusing about them. You see, they will be so far away, so safely done with; never, anyhow, going to happen again. Why of course in time, in years and years, one's troubles must end by being entertaining. But I don't believe, however old I am and however wisely hilarious, I shall ever be able to avoid the stab in the back, the clutch of pain at the heart, that the remembrance of beautiful past happiness gives one. Lost. Lost. Gone. And one is still alive, and still gets up carefully every day, and buttons all one's buttons, and goes down to breakfast.

July 31st.

Once I knew a bishop rather intimately—oh, nothing that wasn't most creditable to us both—and he said to me, 'Dear child, you will always be happy if you are good.'

3

I'm afraid he couldn't have been quite candid, or else he was very inexperienced, for I have never been so terribly good in the bishop's sense as these last three years, turning my back on every private wish, dreadfully unselfish, devoted, a perfect monster of goodness. And unhappiness went with me every step of the way.

I much prefer what some one else said to me, (not a bishop but yet wise,) to whom I commented once on the really extraordinary bubbling happiness that used to wake up with me every morning, the amazing joy of each day as it came, the warm flooding gratitude that I *should* be so happy,—this was before the war. He said, beginning also like the bishop but, unlike him, failing in delicacy at the end, 'Dear child, it is because you have a sound stomach.'

August 1st.

The last first of August I was here was the 1914 one. It was just such a day as this,—blue, hot, glorious of colour and light. We in this house, cut off in our remoteness from the noise and excitement of a world setting out with cries of enthusiasm on its path of suicide, cut off by distance and steepness even from the valley where the dusty Swiss soldiers were collecting and every sort of rumour ran like flames, went as usual through our pleasant day, reading, talking, clambering in the pine-woods, eating romantic meals out in the little garden that hangs like a fringe of flowers along the edge of the rock, unconscious, serene, confident in life. Just as to-day the delphiniums stood brilliantly blue, straight, and motionless on this edge, and it might have been the very same purple pansies crowding at their feet. Nobody came to tell us anything. We were lapped in peace. Of course even up here there had been the slight ruffle of the Archduke's murder in June, and the slight wonder towards the end of July as to what would come of it; but the ruffle and the wonder died away in what seemed the solid, ever-enduring comfortableness of life. Such comfortableness went too deep, was too much settled, too heavy, to make it thinkable that it should ever really be disturbed. There would be quarrels, but they would be localised. Why, the mere feeding of the vast modern armies would etc., etc. We were very innocent and trustful in those days. Looking back at it, it is so pathetic as to be almost worthy of tears.

Well, I don't want to remember all that. One turns with a sick weariness from the recollection. At least one is thankful that we're at Now and not at Then. This first of August has the great advantage of having all that was coming after that first of August behind it instead of ahead of it. At least on this first of August most of the killing, of the slaughtering of young bodies and bright hopes, has left off. The world is very horrible still, but nothing can ever be so horrible as killing.

August 2nd.

The only thing to do with one's old sorrows is to tuck them up neatly in their shroud and turn one's face away from their grave towards what is coming next.

That is what I am going to do. To-day I have the kind of feelings that take hold of convalescents. I hardly dare hope it, but I have done things to-day that do seem convalescent; done them and liked doing them; things that I haven't till to-day had the faintest desire to do.

I've been for a walk. And a quite good walk, up in the forest where the water tumbles over rocks and the air is full of resin. And then when I got home I burrowed about among my books, arranging their volumes and loving the feel of them. It is more than ten days since I got here, and till to-day I haven't moved; till to-day I've lain about with no wish to move, with no wish at all except to have no wish. Once or twice I have been ashamed of myself; and once or twice into the sleepy twilight of my mind has come a little flicker of suspicion that perhaps life still, after all, may be beautiful, that it may perhaps, after all, be just as beautiful as ever if only I will open my eyes and look. But the flicker has soon gone out again, damped out by the vault-like atmosphere of the place it had got into.

To-day I do feel different; and oh how glad I'd be if I *could* be glad! I don't believe there was ever anybody who loved being happy as much as I did. What I mean is that I was so acutely conscious of being happy, so appreciative of it; that I wasn't ever bored, and was always and continuously grateful for the whole delicious loveliness of the world.

I think it must be unusual never to have been bored. I realise this when I hear other people talk. Certainly I'm never bored as people sometimes appear to be by being alone, by the absence of amusement from without; and as for bores, persons who obviously were bores, they didn't bore me, they interested me. It was so wonderful to me, their unawareness that they were bores. Besides, they were usually very kind; and also, shameful though it is to confess, bores like me, and I am touched by being liked, even by a bore. Sometimes it is true I have had to take temporary refuge in doing what Dr. Johnson found so convenient, — withdrawing my attention, but this is dangerous because of the inevitable accompanying glazed and wandering eye. Still, much can be done by practice in combining coherency of response with private separate meditation.

Just before I left London I met a man whose fate it has been for years to sit daily in the Law Courts delivering judgments, and he told me that he took a volume of poetry with him—preferably Wordsworth—and read in it as it lay open on his knees under the table, to the great refreshment and invigoration of his soul; and yet, so skilled had he become in the practice of two attentivenesses, he never missed a word that was said or a point that was made. There are indeed nice people in the world. I did like that man. It seemed such a wise and pleasant thing to do, to lay the dust of those sad places, where people who once liked each other go because they are angry, with the gentle waters of poetry. I am sure that man is the sort of husband whose wife's heart gives a jump of gladness each time he comes home.

August 3rd.

These burning August days, when I live in so great a glory of light and colour that it is like living in the glowing heart of a jewel, how impossible it is to keep from gratitude. I'm so grateful to be here, to *have* here to come to. Really I think I'm beginning to feel different— remote from the old unhappy things that were strangling me dead; restored; almost as though I might really some day be in tune again. There's a moon now, and in the evenings I get into a coat and lie in the low chair in the doorway watching it, and sometimes I forget for as long as a whole half hour that the happiness I believed in is gone for ever. I love sitting there and feeling little gusts of scent cross my face every now and then, as if some one had patted it softly in passing by. Sometimes it is the scent of the cut grass that has been baking all day in the sun, but most often it is the scent from a group of Madonna lilies just outside the door, planted by Antoine in one of the Septembers of the war.

'*C'est ma maman qui me les a donnés,*' he said; and when I had done expressing my joy at their beauty and their fragrance, and my appreciation of his *maman's* conduct in having made my garden so lovely a present, he said that she had given them in order that, by brewing their leaves and applying the resulting concoction at the right moment, he and Mrs. Antoine might be cured of suppurating wounds.

'But you haven't got any suppurating wounds,' I said, astonished and disillusioned.

'*Ah, pour ça non,*' said Antoine. '*Mais il ne faut pas attendre qu'on les a pour se procurer le remède.*'

Well, if he approaches every future contingency with the same prudence he must be kept very busy; but the long winters of the war up here have developed in him, I suppose, a Swiss Family Robinson-like ingenuity of preparation for eventualities.

What lovely long words I've just been writing. I can't be as convalescent as I thought. I'm sure real vigour is brief. You don't say Damn if your vitality is low; you trail among querulous, water-blooded words like regrettable and unfortunate. But I think, perhaps, being in my top layers very adaptable, it was really the elderly books I've been reading the last day or two that made me arrange my language along their lines. Not old books,—elderly. Written in the great Victorian age, when the emotions draped themselves chastely in lengths, and avoided the rude simplicities of shorts.

There is the oddest lot of books in this house, pitchforked together by circumstances, and sometimes their accidental rearrangement by Antoine after cleaning their shelves each spring of my absence would make their writers, if they could know, curdle between their own covers. Some are standing on their heads—Antoine has no prejudices about the right side up of an author—most of those in sets have their volumes wrong, and yesterday I found a Henry James, lost from the rest of him, lost even, it looked like, to propriety, held tight between two ladies. The ladies were Ouida and Ella Wheeler Wilcox. They would hardly let him go, they had got him so tight. I pulled him out, a little damaged, and restored him, ruffled in spite of my careful smoothing, to his proper place. It was the *Son and Brother*, and there he had been for months, perhaps years, being hugged. Dreadful.

When I come down to breakfast and find I am a little ahead of the *café au lait*, I wander into the place that has most books in it—though indeed books are in every place, and have even oozed along the passages—and fill up the time, till Mrs. Antoine calls me, in rescue work of an urgent nature. But it is impossible, I find, to tidy books without ending by sitting on the floor in the middle of a great untidiness and reading. The coffee grows cold and the egg repulsive, but still I read. You open a book idly, and you see:

The most glaring anomalies seemed to afford them no intellectual inconvenience, neither would they listen to any arguments as to the waste of money and happiness which their folly caused them. I was allowed almost to call them life-long self-deceivers to their faces, and they said it was quite true, but that it did not matter.

Naturally then you read on.

You open another book idly, and you see:

Our admiration of King Alfred is greatly increased by the fact that we know very little about him.

Naturally then you read on.

You open another book idly, and you see:

Organic life, we are told, has developed gradually from the protozoon to the philosopher, and this development, we are assured, is indubitably an advance. Unfortunately it is the philosopher, not the protozoon, who gives us this assurance.

Naturally then you read on.

You open—but I could go on all day like this, as I do go on being caught among the books, and only the distant anxious chirps of Mrs. Antoine, who comes round to the front door to clear away breakfast and finds it hasn't been begun, can extricate me.

Perhaps I had better not get arranging books before breakfast. It is too likely to worry that bird-like Mrs. Antoine, who is afraid, I daresay, that if I don't drink my coffee while it is hot I may relapse into that comatose condition that filled her evidently with much uneasiness and awe. She hadn't expected, I suppose, the mistress of the house, when she did at last get back to it, to behave like some strange alien slug, crawled up the mountain only to lie motionless in the sun for the best part of a fortnight. I heard her, after the first two days of this conduct, explaining it to Antoine, who however needed no explanation because of his god-like habit of never being surprised, and her explanation was that *c'était la guerre,*—convenient explanation that has been used to excuse many more unnatural and horrible things during the last five years than somebody's behaving as if she were a slug.

But, really, the accidental juxtapositions on my bookshelves! Just now I found George Moore (his *Memories of my Dead Life*, with its delicate unmoralities, its delicious paganism) with on one side of him a book called *Bruey: a Little Worker for Christ*, by Frances Ridley Havergal, and on the other an American book called *The Unselfishness of God, and How I Discovered It*.

The surprise of finding these three with their arms, as it were, round each other's necks, got me nearer to laughter than I have been for months. If anybody had been with me I *would* have laughed. Is it possible that I am so far on to-day in convalescence that I begin to want a companion? Somebody to laugh with? Why, if that is so....

But I'd best not be too hopeful.

August 4th.

This day five years ago! What a thrill went through us up here, how proud we felt of England, of belonging to England; proud with that extraordinary intensified patriotism that lays hold of those who are not in their own country.

It is very like the renewal of affection, the re-flaming up of love, for the absent. The really wise are often absent; though, indeed, their absences should be arranged judiciously. Too much absence is very nearly as bad as too little,—no, not really very nearly; I should rather say too much has its drawbacks too, though only at first. Persisted in these drawbacks turn into merits; for doesn't absence, prolonged enough, lead in the end to freedom? I suppose, however, for most people complete freedom is too lonely a thing, therefore the absence should only be just long enough to make room for one to see clear again. Just a little withdrawal every now and then, just a little, so as to get a good view once more of those dear qualities we first loved, so as to be able to see that they're still there, still shining.

How can you see anything if your nose is right up against it? I know when we were in England, enveloped in her life at close quarters, bewildered by the daily din of the newspapers, stunned by the cries of the politicians, distracted by the denouncements, accusations, revilings with which the air was convulsed, and acutely aware of the background of sad drizzling rain on the pavements, and of places like Cromwell Road and Shaftesbury Avenue and Ashley Gardens being there all the time, never different, great ugly houses with the rain dripping on them, gloomy temporary lodgings for successive processions of the noisy dead,—I know when we were in the middle of all this, right up tight against it, we couldn't see, and so we forgot the side of England that was great.

But when she went to war we were not there; we had been out of her for months, and she had got focussed again patriotically. Again she was the precious stone set in a silver sea, the other Eden, demi-Paradise, the England my England, the splendid thing that had made splendid poets, the hope and heart of the world. Long before she had buckled on her sword—how easily one drops into the old language!—long before there was any talk of war, just by sheer being away from her we had re-acquired that peculiar aggressive strut of the spirit that is patriotism. We liked the Swiss, we esteemed them; and when we crossed into Italy we liked the Italians too, though esteeming them less,—I think because they seemed less thrifty and enjoyed themselves more, and we were still sealed up in the old opinion that undiscriminating joyless thrift was virtuous. But though we liked and esteemed these people it was from a height. At the back of our minds we always felt superior, at the back of our minds we were strutting. Every day of further absence from England, our England, increased that delicious sub-conscious smugness. Then when on the 4th of August she 'came in,' came in gloriously because of her word to Belgium, really this little house contained so much enthusiasm and pride that it almost could be heard cracking.

What shall we do when we all get to heaven and aren't allowed to have any patriotism? There, surely, we shall at last be forced into one vast family. But I imagine that every time God isn't looking the original patriotism of each will break out, right along throughout eternity; and some miserable English tramp, who has only been let into heaven because he positively wasn't man enough for hell, will seize his opportunity to hiss at a neat Swiss business man from Berne, whose life on earth was blamelessly spent in the production of cuckoo-clocks, and whose mechanical-ingenuity was such that he even, so ran the heavenly rumours among the mild, astonished angels, had propagated his family by machinery, that he, the tramp, is a b—Briton, and if he, the b—b—b—Swiss (I believe tramps always talk in b's; anyhow newspapers and books say they do), doubts it, he'd b— well better come outside and he, the tramp, will b—well soon show him.

To which the neat Berne gentleman, on other subjects so completely pervaded by the local heavenly calm, will answer with a sudden furious mechanical buzzing, much worse and much more cowing to the tramp than any swear-words, and passionately uphold the might and majesty of Switzerland in a prolonged terrific*whrrrr*.

August 5th.

I want to talk. I must be better.

August 6th.

Of course, the most battered, the most obstinately unhappy person couldn't hold out for ever against the all-pervading benediction of this place. I know there is just the same old wretchedness going on as usual outside it,—cruelty, people wantonly making each other miserable, love being thrown away or frightened into fits, the dreadful betrayal of trust that is the blackest wretchedness of all,—I can almost imagine that if I were to hang over my terrace-wall I would see these well-known dreary horrors crawling about in the valley below, crawling and tumbling about together in a ghastly tangle. But at least there isn't down there now my own particular contribution to the general wretchedness. I brought that up here; dragged it up with me, not because I wanted to, but because it would come. Surely, though, I shall leave it here? Surely there'll be a day when I'll be able to pack it away into a neat bundle and take it up to the top of some, arid, never-again-to-be-visited rock, and leave it there and say, 'Goodbye. I'm separate. I've cut the umbilical cord. Goodbye old misery. Now for what comes next.'

I can't believe this won't happen. I can't believe I won't go back down the mountain different from what I was when I came. Lighter, anyhow, and more wholesome inside. Oh, I do so *want* to be wholesome inside again! Nicely aired, sunshiny; instead of all dark, and stuffed up with black memories.

August 7th.

But I am getting on. Every morning now when I wake and see the patch of bright sunshine on the wall at the foot of my bed that means another perfect day, my heart goes out in an eager prayer that I may not disgrace so great a blessing by private gloom. And I do think each of these last days has been a little less disgraced than its yesterday. Hardly a smudge, for instance, has touched any part of this afternoon. I have felt as though indeed I were at last sitting up and taking notice. And the first thing I want to do, the first use I want to make of having turned the corner, is to talk.

How feminine. But I love to talk. Again how feminine. Well, I also love to listen. But chiefly I love to listen to a man; therefore once more, how feminine. Well, I'm a woman, so naturally I'm feminine; and a man does seem to have more to say that one wants to hear than a woman. I do want to hear what a woman has to say too, but not for so long a time, and not so often. Not nearly so often. What reason to give for this reluctance I don't quite know, except that a woman when she talks seems usually to have forgotten the salt. Also she is apt to go on talking; sometimes for quite a little while after you have begun to wish she would leave off.

One of the last people who stayed here with me alone in 1914, just before the arrival of the gay holiday group of the final days, was a woman of many gifts—*le trop est l'ennemi du bien*—who started, therefore, being full of these gifts and having eloquently to let them out, talking at the station in the valley where I met her, and didn't, to my growing amazement and chagrin, for I too wanted to say some things, leave off (except when night wrapped her up in blessed silence) till ten days afterwards, when by the mercy of providence she swallowed a crumb wrong, and so had to stop.

How eagerly, released for a moment, I rushed in with as much as I could get out during the brief time I knew she would take to recover! But my voice, hoarse with disuse, had hardly said three sentences—miserable little short ones—when she did recover, and fixing impatient and reproachful eyes on me said:

'Do you *always* talk so much?'

Surely that was unjust?

August 8th.

Now see what Henry James wrote to me—to *me* if you please! I can't get over it, such a feather in my cap. Why, I had almost forgotten I had a cap to have a feather in, so profound has been my humbling since last I was here.

In the odd, fairy-tale like way I keep on finding bits of the past, of years ago, as though they were still of the present, even of the last half hour, I found the letter this morning in a room I wandered into after breakfast. It is the only room downstairs besides the hall, and I used to take refuge in it from the other gay inhabitants of the house so as to open and answer letters somewhere not too distractingly full of cheerful talk; and there on the table, spotlessly kept clean by Antoine but else not touched, were all the papers and odds and ends of five years back exactly as I must have left them. Even some chocolate I had apparently been eating, and some pennies, and a handful of cigarettes, and actually a box of matches,—it was all there, all beautifully dusted, all as it must have been when last I sat there at the table. If it hadn't been for the silence, the complete, sunny emptiness and silence of the house, I would certainly have thought I had only been asleep and having a bad dream, and that not five years but one uneasy night had gone since I nibbled that chocolate and wrote with those pens.

Fascinated and curious I sat down and began eating the chocolate again. It was quite good; made of good, lasting stuff in that good, apparently lasting age we used to live in. And while I ate it I turned over the piles of papers, and there at the bottom of them was a letter from Henry James.

8

I expect I kept it near me on the table because I so much loved it and wanted to re-read it, and wanted, I daresay, at intervals proudly to show it to my friends and make them envious, for it was written at Christmas, 1913; months before I left for England.

Reading it now my feeling is just astonishment that I, I should ever have had such a letter. But then I am greatly humbled; I have been on the rocks; and can't believe that such a collection of broken bits as I am now could ever have been a trim bark with all its little sails puffed out by the kindliness and affection of anybody as wonderful as Henry James.

Here it is; and it isn't any more vain of me now in my lamed and bruised condition to copy it out and hang on its charming compliments than it is vain for a woman who once was lovely and is now grown old to talk about how pretty she used to be:

21   Carlyle   Mansions,

Cheyne   Walk,   S.W.,

December 29th, 1913.

Dear—

Let me tell you that I simply delight in your beautiful and generous and gracious little letter, and that there isn't a single honeyed word of it that doesn't give me the most exquisite pleasure. You fill the measure—and how can I tell you how I *like* the measure to be filled? None of your quarter-bushels or half-bushels for *my* insatiable appetite, but the overflowing heap, pressed down and shaken together and spilling all over the place. So I pick up the golden grains and nibble them one by one! Truly, dear lady, it is the charmingest rosy flower of a letter—handed me straight out of your monstrous snowbank. That you can grow such flowers in such conditions—besides growing with such diligence and elegance all sorts of other lovely kinds, has for its explanation of course only that you have such a regular teeming garden of a mind. You must mainly inhabit it of course—with your other courts of exercise so grand, if you will, but so grim. Well, you have caused me to revel in pride and joy—for I assure you that I have let myself go; all the more that the revelry of the season here itself has been so far from engulfing me that till your witching words came I really felt perched on a mountain of lonely bleakness socially and sensuously speaking alike—very much like one of those that group themselves, as I suppose, under your windows. But I have had my Xmastide *now*, and am your all grateful and faithful and all unforgetting old Henry James.

Who wouldn't be proud of getting a letter like that? It was wonderful to come across it again, wonderful how my chin went up in the air and how straight I sat up for a bit after reading it. And I laughed, too; for with what an unbuttoned exuberance must I have engulfed him! 'Spilling all over the place.' I can quite believe it. I had, I suppose, been reading or re-reading something of his, and had been swept off sobriety of expression by delight, and in that condition of emotional unsteadiness and molten appreciation must have rushed impetuously to the nearest pen.

How warmly, with what grateful love, one thinks of Henry James. How difficult to imagine anyone riper in wisdom, in kindliness, in wit; greater of affection; more generous of friendship. And his talk, his wonderful talk,—even more wonderful than his books. If only he had had a Boswell! I did ask him one day, in a courageous after-dinner mood, if he wouldn't take me on as his Boswell; a Boswell so deeply devoted that perhaps qualifications for the post would grow through sheer admiration. I told him—my courageous levity was not greater on that occasion than his patience—that I would disguise myself as a man; or better still, not being quite big enough to make a plausible man and unlikely to grow any more except, it might be hoped, in grace, I would be an elderly boy; that I would rise up early and sit up late and learn shorthand and do anything in the world, if only I might trot about after him taking notes—the strange pair we should have made! And the judgment he passed on that reckless suggestion, after considering its impudence with much working about of his extraordinary mobile mouth, delivering his verdict with a weight of pretended self-depreciation intended to crush me speechless,—which it did for nearly a whole second—was: 'Dear lady, it would be like the slow squeezing out of a big empty sponge.'

9

August 9th.

This little wooden house, clinging on to the side of the mountain by its eyelashes, or rather by its eyebrows, for it has enormous eaves to protect it from being smothered in winter in snow that look exactly like overhanging eyebrows,—is so much cramped up for room to stand on that the garden along the edge of the rock isn't much bigger than a handkerchief.

It is a strip of grass, tended with devotion by Antoine, whose pride it is that it should be green when all the other grass on the slopes round us up the mountain and down the mountain are parched pale gold; which leads him to spend most of his evening hours watering it. There is a low wall along the edge to keep one from tumbling over, for if one did tumble over it wouldn't be nice for the people walking about in the valley five thousand feet below, and along this wall is the narrow ribbon of the only flowers that will put up with us.

They aren't many. There are the delphiniums, and some pansies and some pinks, and a great many purple irises. The irises were just over when I first got here, but judging from the crowds of flower-stalks they must have been very beautiful. There is only one flower left; exquisite and velvety and sun-warmed to kiss—which I do diligently, for one must kiss something—and with that adorable honey-smell that is the very smell of summer.

That's all in the garden. It isn't much, written down, but you should just see it. Oh yes—I forgot. Round the corner, scrambling up the wall that protects the house in the early spring from avalanches, are crimson ramblers, brilliant against the intense blue of the sky. Crimson ramblers are, I know, ordinary things, but you should just see them. It is the colour of the sky that makes them so astonishing here. Yes—and I forgot the lilies that Antoine's *maman* gave him. They are near the front door, and next to them is a patch of lavender in full flower now, and all day long on each of its spikes is poised miraculously something that looks like a tiny radiant angel, but that flutters up into the sun when I go near and is a white butterfly. Antoine must have put in the lavender. It used not to be there. But I don't ask him because of what he might tell me it is really for, and I couldn't bear to have that patch of sheer loveliness, with the little shining things hovering over it, explained as a *remède* for something horrid.

If I could paint I would sit all day and paint; as I can't I try to get down on paper what I see. It gives me pleasure. It is somehow companionable. I wouldn't, I think, do this if I were not alone. I would probably exhaust myself and my friend pointing out the beauty.

The garden, it will be seen, as gardens go, is pathetic in its smallness and want of variety. Possessors of English gardens, with those immense wonderful herbaceous borders and skilfully arranged processions of flowers, might conceivably sniff at it. Let them. I love it. And, if it were smaller still, if it were shrunk to a single plant with a single flower on it, it would perhaps only enchant me the more, for then I would concentrate on that one beauty and not be distracted by the feeling that does distract me here, that while I am looking one way I am missing what is going on in other directions. Those beasts in Revelations—the ones full of eyes before and behind—I wish I had been constructed on liberal principles like that.

But one really hardly wants a garden here where God does so much. It is like Italy in that way, and an old wooden box of pansies or a pot of lilies stuck anywhere, in a window, on the end of a wall, is enough; composing instantly with what is so beautifully there already, the light, the colour, the shapes of the mountains. Really, where God does it all for you just a yard or two arranged in your way is enough; enough to assert your independence, and to show a proper determination to make something of your own.

August 10th.

I don't know when it is most beautiful up here,—in the morning, when the heat lies along the valley in delicate mists, and the folded mountains, one behind the other, grow dimmer and dimmer beyond sight, swooning away through tender gradations of violets and greys, or at night when I look over the edge of the terrace and see the lights in the valley shimmering as though they were reflected in water.

I seem to be seeing it now for the first time, with new eyes. I know I used to see it when I was here before, used to feel it and rejoice in it, but it was entangled in other things then, it was only part of the many happinesses with which those days were full, claiming my

10

attention and my thoughts. They claimed them wonderfully and hopefully it is true, but they took me much away from what I can only call for want of a better word—(a better word: what a thing to say!)—God. Now those hopes and wonders, those other joys and lookings-forward and happy trusts are gone; and the wounds they left, the dreadful sore places, are slowly going too. And how I see beauty now is with the new sensitiveness, the new astonishment at it, of a person who for a long time has been having awful dreams, and one morning wakes up and the delirium is gone, and he lies in a state of the most exquisite glad thankfulness, the most extraordinary minute appreciation of the dear, wonderful common things of life,—just the sun shining on his counterpane, the scents from the garden coming in through his window, the very smell of the coffee being got ready for breakfast. Oh, delight, delight to think one didn't die this time, that one isn't going to die this time after all, but is going to get better, going to live, going presently to be quite well again and able to go back to one's friends, to the people who still love one....

August 11th.

To-day is a saint's day. This is a Catholic part of Switzerland, and they have a great many holidays because they have a great many saints. There is hardly a week without some saint in it who has to be commemorated, and often there are two in the same week, and sometimes three. I know when we have reached another saint, for then the church bells of the nearest village begin to jangle, and go on doing it every two hours. When this happens the peasants leave off work, and the busy, saint-unencumbered Protestants get ahead.

Mrs. Antoine was a Catholic before she married, but the sagacious Antoine, who wasn't one, foreseeing days in most of his weeks when she might, if he hadn't been quite kind, to her, or rather if she fancied he hadn't been quite kind to her—and the fancies of wives, he had heard, were frequent and vivid—the sagacious Antoine, foreseeing these numerous holy days ahead of him on any of which Mrs. Antoine might explain as piety what was really pique and decline to cook his dinner, caused her to turn Protestant before the wedding. Which she did; conscious, as she told me, that she was getting a *bon mari qui valait bien ça;* and thus at one stroke Antoine secured his daily dinners throughout the year and rid himself of all his wife's relations. For they, consisting I gather principally of aunts, her father and mother being dead, were naturally displeased and won't know the Antoines; which is, I am told by those who have managed it, the most refreshing thing in the world: to get your relations not to know you. So that not only does he live now in the blessed freedom and dignity that appears to be reserved for those whose relations are angry, but he has no priests about him either. Really Antoine is very intelligent.

And he has done other intelligent things while I have been away. For instance:

When first I came here, two or three years before the war, I desired to keep the place free from the smells of farmyards. 'There shall be no cows,' I said.

'*C'est bien,*' said Antoine.

'Nor any chickens.'

'*C'est bien*' said Antoine.

'Neither shall there be any pigs.'

'*C'est bien,*' said Antoine.

'*Surtout,*' I repeated, fancying I saw in his eye a kind of private piggy regret, '*pas de porcs.*'

'*C'est bien,*' said Antoine, the look fading.

For most of my life up to then had been greatly infested by pigs; and though they were superior pigs, beautifully kept, housed and fed far better, shameful to relate, than the peasants of that place, on the days when the wind blew from where they were to where we were, clean them and air them as one might there did come blowing over us a great volume of unmistakeable pig. Eclipsing the lilies. Smothering the roses. Also, on still days we could hear their voices, and the calm of many a summer evening was rent asunder by their squeals. There were an enormous number of little pigs, for in that part of the country it was unfortunately not the custom to eat sucking-pigs, which is such a convenient as well as agreeable way of keeping them quiet, and they squealed atrociously; out of sheer high spirits, I suppose, being pampered pigs and having no earthly reason to squeal except for joy.

Remembering all this, I determined that up here at any rate we should be pure from pigs. And from cows too; and from chickens. For did I not also remember things both cows and chickens had done to me? The hopes of a whole year in the garden had often been destroyed by one absent-minded, wandering cow; and though we did miracles with wire-netting and the concealing of wire-netting by creepers, sooner or later a crowd of lustful hens, led by some great bully of a cock, got in and tore up the crocuses just at that early time of the year when, after an endless winter, crocuses seem the most precious and important things in the world.

Therefore this place had been kept carefully empty of live-stock, and we bought our eggs and our milk from the peasants, and didn't have any sausages, and the iris bulbs were not scratched up, and the air had nothing in it but smells of honey and hay in summer, and nothing in winter but the ineffable pure cold smell of what, again for want of a better word, I can only describe as God. But then the war came, and our hurried return to England; and instead of being back as we had thought for Christmas, we didn't come back at all. Year after year went, Christmas after Christmas, and nobody came back. I suppose Antoine began at last to feel as if nobody ever would come back. I can't guess at what moment precisely in those years his thoughts began to put out feelers towards pigs, but he did at last consider it proper to regard my pre-war instructions as finally out of date, and gathered a suitable selection of live-stock about him. I expect he got to this stage fairly early, for having acquired a nice, round little wife he was determined, being a wise man, to keep her so. And having also an absentee *patrone*—that is the word that locally means me—absent, and therefore not able to be disturbed by live-stock, he would keep her placid by keeping her unconscious.

How simple, and how intelligent.

In none of his monthly letters did the word pig, cow, or chicken appear. He wrote agreeably of the weather: *c'était magnifique,* or *c'était bien triste,* according to the season. He wrote of the French and Belgian sick prisoners of war, interned in those places scattered about the mountains which used to be the haunts of parties catered for by Lunn. He wrote appreciatively of the usefulness and good conduct of the watch-dog, a splendid creature, much bigger than I am, with the lap-doggy name of Mou-Mou. He lengthily described unexciting objects like the whiskers of the cat:*favoris superbes qui poussent toujours, malgré ces jours maigres de guerre;* and though sometimes he expressed a little disappointment at the behaviour of Mrs. Antoine's *estomac, qui lui fait beaucoup d'ennuis et paraît mal résister aux grands froids,* he always ended up soothingly: *Pour la maison tout va bien. Madame peut être entièrement tranquille.*

Never a word, you see, about the live-stock.

So there in England was Madame being *entièrement tranquille* about her little house, and glad indeed that she could be; for whatever had happened to it or to the Antoines she wouldn't have been able to do anything. Tethered on the other side of the impassable barrier of war, if the house had caught fire she could only, over there in England, have wrung her hands; and if Mrs. Antoine's *estomac* had given out so completely that she and Antoine had to abandon their post and take to the plains and doctors, she could only have sat still and cried. The soothing letters were her comfort for five years,—*madame peût-être entièrement tranquille;* how sweetly the words fell, month by month, on ears otherwise harassed and tormented!

It wasn't till I had been here nearly a fortnight that I began to be aware of my breakfast. Surely it was very nice? Such a lot of milk; and every day a little jug of cream. And surprising butter,—surprising not only because it was so very fresh but because it was there at all. I had been told in England that there was no butter to be got here, not an ounce to be bought from one end of Switzerland to the other. Well, there it was; fresh every day, and in a singular abundance.

Through the somnolence of my mind, of all the outward objects surrounding me I think it was the butter that got in first; and my awakening intelligence, after a period of slow feeling about and some relapses, did at last one morning hit on the conviction that at the other end of that butter was a cow.

This, so far, was to be expected as the result of reasoning. But where I began to be pleased with myself, and feel as if Paley's Evidences had married Sherlock Holmes and I was

12

the bright pledge of their loves, was when I proceeded from this, without moving from my chair, to discover by sheer thinking that the cow was very near the butter, because else the butter couldn't possibly be made fresh every day,—so near that it must be at that moment grazing on the bit of pasture belonging to me; and, if that were so, the conclusion was irresistible that it must be my cow.

After that my thoughts leaped about the breakfast table with comparative nimbleness. I remembered that each morning there had been an egg, and that eggy puddings had appeared at the other meals. Before the war it was almost impossible to get eggs up here; clearly, then, I had chickens of my own. And the honey; I felt it would no longer surprise me to discover that I also had bees, for this honey was the real thing,—not your made-up stuff of the London shops. And strawberries; every morning a great cabbage leaf of strawberries had been on the table, real garden strawberries, over long ago down in the valley and never dreamed of as things worth growing by the peasants in the mountains. Obviously I counted these too among my possessions in some corner out of sight. The one object I couldn't proceed to by inductive reasoning from what was on the table was a pig. Antoine's courage had failed him over that. Too definitely must my repeated warning have echoed in his ears: *Surtout pas de porcs.*

But how very intelligent he had been. It needs intelligence if one is conscientious to disobey orders at the right moment. And me so unaware all the time, and therefore so unworried!

He passed along the terrace at that moment, a watering-pot in his hand.

'Antoine,' I said.

'Madame,' he said, stopping and taking off his cap.

'This egg—' I said, pointing to the shell. I said it in French, but prefer not to put my French on paper.

'*Ah—madame a vu les poules.*'

'This butter—'

'*Ah—madame a visité la vache.*'

'The pig—?' I hesitated. 'Is there—is there also a pig?'

'*Si madame veut descendre à la cave—*'

'You never keep a pig in the cellar?' I exclaimed.

'*Comme jambon,*' said Antoine—calm, perfect of manner, without a trace of emotion.

And there sure enough I was presently proudly shown by Mrs. Antoine, whose feelings are less invisible than her husband's, hanging from the cellar ceiling on hooks that which had once been pig. Several pigs; though she talked as if there had never been more than one. It may be so, of course, but if it is so it must have had a great many legs.

Un porc centipède, I remarked thoughtfully, gazing upwards at the forest of hams.

Over the thin ice of this comment she slid, however, in a voluble description of how, when the armistice was signed, she and Antoine had instantly fallen upon and slain the pig— pig still in the singular—expecting Madame's arrival after that felicitous event at any minute, and comprehending that *un porc vivant pourrait déranger madame, mais que mort il ne fait rien à personne que du plaisir.* And she too gazed upwards, but with affection and pride.

There remained then nothing to do but round off these various transactions by a graceful and grateful paying for them. Which I did to-day, Antoine presenting the bills, accompanied by complicated calculations and deductions of the market price of the milk and butter and eggs he and Mrs. Antoine would otherwise have consumed during the past years.

I didn't look too closely into what the pig had cost,—his price, as my eye skimmed over it was obviously the price of something plural. But my eye only skimmed. It didn't dwell. Always Antoine and I have behaved to each other like gentlemen.

August 12th.

I wonder why I write all this. Is it because it is so like talking to a friend at the end of the day, and telling him, who is interested and loves to hear, everything one has done? I suppose it is that; and that I want, besides, to pin down these queer days as they pass,—days so utterly unlike any I ever had before. I want to hold them a minute in my hand and look at them, before letting them drop away for ever. Then, perhaps, in lots of years, when I have half forgotten what brought me up here, and don't mind a bit about anything except to laugh—to laugh with the tenderness of a wise old thing at the misunderstandings, and mistakes, and failures that brought me so near shipwreck, and yet underneath were still somehow packed with love—I'll open this and read it, and I daresay quote that Psalm about going through the vale of misery and using it as a well, and be quite pleasantly entertained.

August 13th.

If one sets one's face westwards and goes on and on along the side of the mountain, refusing either to climb higher or go lower, and having therefore to take things as they come and somehow get through—roaring torrents, sudden ravines, huge trees blown down in a forgotten blizzard and lying right across one's way; all the things that mountains have up their sleeve waiting for one—one comes, after two hours of walk so varied as to include scowling rocks and gloomy forests, bright stretches of delicious grass full of flowers, bits of hayfield, clusters of fruit-trees, wide sun-flooded spaces with nothing between one apparently and the great snowy mountains, narrow paths where it is hardly light enough to see, smells of resin and hot fir needles, smells of traveller's joy, smells of just cut grass, smells of just sawn wood, smells of water tumbling over stones, muddy smells where the peasants have turned some of the torrent away through shallow channels into their fields, honey smells, hot smells, cold smells,—after two hours of this walking, which would be tiring because of the constant difficulty of the ground if it weren't for the odd way the air has here of carrying you, of making you feel as though you were being lifted along, one comes at last to the edge of a steep slope where there is a little group of larches.

Then one sits down.

These larches are at the very end of a long tongue into which the mountain one started on has somehow separated, and it is under them that one eats one's dinner of hard boiled egg and bread and butter, and sits staring, while one does so, in much astonishment at the view. For it is an incredibly beautiful view from here, of an entirely different range of mountains from the one seen from my terrace; and the valley, with its twisting, tiny silver thread that I know is a great rushing river, has strange, abrupt, isolated hills scattered over it that appear each to have a light and colour of its own, with no relation to the light and colour of the mountains.

When first I happened on this place the building of my house had already been started, and it was too late to run to the architect and say: Here and here only will I live. But I did for a wild moment, so great was the beauty I had found, hope that perhaps Swiss houses might be like those Norwegian ones one reads about that take to pieces and can be put up again somewhere else when you've got bored, and I remember scrambling back hastily in heat and excitement to ask him whether this were so.

He said it wasn't; and seemed even a little ruffled, if so calm a man were capable of ruffling, that I should suppose he would build anything that could come undone.

'This house,' he said, pointing at the hopeless-looking mass that ultimately became so adorable, 'is built for posterity. It is on a rock, and will partake of the same immovability.'

And when I told him of the place I had found, the exquisite place, more beautiful than a dream and a hundred times more beautiful than the place we had started building on, he, being a native of the district, hardy on his legs on Sundays and accordingly acquainted with every inch of ground within twenty miles, told me that it was so remote from villages, so inaccessible by any road, that it was suited as a habitation only to goats.

'Only goats,' he said with finality, waving his hand, 'could dwell there, and for goats I do not build.'

So that my excitement cooled down before the inevitable, and I have lived to be very glad the house is where it is and not where, for a few wild hours, I wanted it; for now I can go to the other when I am in a beauty mood and see it every time with fresh wonder, while if I lived there I would have got used to it long ago, and my ardour been, like other ardours, turned by possession into complacency. Or, to put it a little differently, the house here is like an amiable wife to whom it is comfortable to come back for meals and sleeping purposes, and the other is a secret love, to be visited only on the crest of an ecstasy.

To-day I took a hard boiled egg and some bread and butter, and visited my secret love.

The hard boiled egg doesn't seem much like an ecstasy, but it is a very good foundation for one. There is great virtue in a hard boiled egg. It holds one down, yet not too heavily. It satisfies without inflaming. Sometimes, after days of living on fruit and bread, a slice of underdone meat put in a sandwich and eaten before I knew what I was doing, has gone straight to my head in exactly the way wine would, and I have seen the mountains double and treble themselves, besides not keeping still, in a very surprising and distressing way, utterly ruinous to raptures. So now I distrust sandwiches and will not take them; and all that goes with me is the hard boiled egg. Oh, and apricots, when I can get them. I forgot the apricots. I took a handful to-day,—big, beautiful rosy-golden ones, grown in the hot villages of the valley, a very apricotty place. And, that every part of me should have sustenance, I also took Law's *Serious Call*.

He went because he's the thinnest book I've got on my shelves that has at the same time been praised by Dr. Johnson. I've got several others that Dr. Johnson has praised, such as Ogden on *Prayer*, but their bulk, even if their insides were attractive, makes them have to stay at home. Johnson, I remembered, as I weighed Law thoughtfully in my hand and felt how thin he was, said of the *Serious Call* that he took it up expecting it to be a dull book, and perhaps to laugh at it—'but I found Law quite an overmatch for me.' He certainly would be an overmatch for me, I knew, should I try to stand up to him, but that was not my intention. What I wanted was a slender book that yet would have enough entertainment in it to nourish me all day; and opening the *Serious Call* I was caught at once by the story of Octavius, a learned and ingenious man who, feeling that he wasn't going to live much longer, told the friends hanging on his lips attentive to the wisdom that would, they were sure, drop out, that in the decay of nature in which he found himself he had left off all taverns and was now going to be nice in what he drank, so that he was resolved to furnish his cellar with a little of the very best whatever it might cost. And hardly had he delivered himself of this declaration than 'he fell ill, was committed to a nurse, and had his eyes closed by her before his fresh parcel of wine came in.'

The effect of this on some one called Eugenius was to send him home a new man, full of resolutions to devote himself wholly to God; for 'I never, says Eugenius, was so deeply affected with the wisdom and importance of religion as when I saw how poorly and meanly the learned Octavius was to leave the world through the want of it.'

So Law went with me, and his vivacious pages,—the story of Octavius is but one of many; there is Matilda and her unhappy daughters ('The eldest daughter lived as long as she could under this discipline,' but found she couldn't after her twentieth year and died, 'her entrails much hurt by being crushed together with her stays';) Eusebia and her happy daughters, who were so beautifully brought up that they had the satisfaction of dying virgins; Lepidus, struck down as he was dressing himself for a feast; the admirable Miranda, whose meals were carefully kept down to exactly enough to give her proper strength to lift eyes and hands to heaven, so that 'Miranda will never have her eyes swell with fatness or pant under a heavy load of flesh until she has changed her religion'; Mundamus, who if he saw a book of devotion passed it by; Classicus, who openly and shamelessly preferred learning to devotion—these vivacious pages greatly enlivened and adorned my day. But I did feel, as I came home at the end of it, that Dr. Johnson, for whom no one has more love and less respect than I, ought to have spent some at least of his earlier years, when he was still accessible to reason, with, say, Voltaire.

Now I am going to bed, footsore but glad, for this picnic to-day was a test. I wanted to see how far on I have got in facing memories. When I set out I pretended to myself that I was going from sheer considerateness for servants, because I wished Mrs. Antoine to have a holiday from cooking my dinner, but I knew in my heart that I was making, in trepidation and secret doubt, a test. For the way to this place of larches bristles with happy memories. They would be sitting waiting for me, I knew, at every bush and corner in radiant rows. If only they wouldn't be radiant, I thought, I wouldn't mind. The way, I thought, would have been easier if it had been punctuated with remembered quarrels. Only then I wouldn't have gone to it at all, for my spirit shudders away from places where there has been unkindness. It is the happy record of this little house that never yet have its walls heard an unkind word or a rude word, and not once has anybody cried in it. All the houses I have lived in, except this, had their sorrows, and one at least had worse things than sorrows; but this one, my little house of peace hung up in the sunshine well on the way to heaven, is completely free from stains, nothing has ever lived in it that wasn't kind. And I shall not count the wretchedness I dragged up with me three weeks ago as a break in this record, as a smudge on its serenity, but only as a shadow passing across the sun. Because, however beaten down I was and miserable, I brought no anger with me and no resentment. Unkindness has still not come into the house.

Now I am going very happy to bed, for I have passed the test. The whole of the walk to the larches, and the whole of the way back, and all the time I was sitting there, what I felt was simply gratitude, gratitude for the beautiful past times I have had. I found I couldn't help it. It was as natural as breathing. I wasn't lonely. Everybody I have loved and shall never see again was with me. And all day, the whole of the wonderful day of beauty, I was able in that bright companionship to forget the immediate grief, the aching wretchedness, that brought me up here to my mountains as a last hope.

August 14th.

To-day it is my birthday, so I thought I would expiate it by doing some useful work.

It is the first birthday I've ever been alone, with nobody to say Bless you. I like being blessed on my birthday, seen off into my new year with encouragement and smiles. Perhaps, I thought, while I dressed, Antoine would remember. After all, I used to have birthdays when I was here before, and he must have noticed the ripple of excitement that lay along the day, how it was wreathed in flowers from breakfast-time on and dotted thick with presents. Perhaps he would remember, and wish me luck. Perhaps if he remembered he would tell his wife, and she would wish me luck too. I did very much long to-day to be wished luck.

But Antoine, if he had ever known, had obviously forgotten. He was doing something to the irises when I came down, and though I went out and lingered round him before beginning breakfast he took no notice; he just went on with the irises. So I daresay I looked a little wry, for I did feel rather afraid I might be going to be lonely.

This, then, I thought, giving myself a hitch of determination, was the moment for manual labour. As I drank my coffee I decided to celebrate the day by giving both the Antoines a holiday and doing the work myself. Why shouldn't my birthday be celebrated by somebody else having a good time? What did it after all matter who had the good time so long as somebody did? The Antoines should have a holiday, and I would work. So would I defend my thoughts from memories that might bite. So would I, by the easy path of perspiration, find peace.

Antoine, however, didn't seem to want a holiday. I had difficulty with him. He wasn't of course surprised when I told him he had got one, because he never is, but he said, with that level intonation that gives his conversation so noticeable a calm, that it was the day for cutting the lawn.

I said I would cut the lawn; I knew about lawns; I had been brought up entirely on lawns,—I believe I told him I had been born on one, in my eagerness to forestall his objections and get him to go.

He said that such work would be too hot for Madame in the sort of weather we were having; and I said that no work on an object so small as our lawn could be too hot. Besides, I liked being hot, I explained—again with eagerness—I wanted to be hot, I was happy when I was hot. '*J'aime beaucoup,* I said, not stopping in my hurry to pick my words, and anyhow imperfect in French, '*la sueur.*'

I believe I ought to have said *la transpiration,* the other word being held in slight if any esteem as a word for ladies, but I still more believe that I oughtn't to have said anything about it at all. I don't know, of course, because of Antoine's immobility of expression; but in spite of this not varying at what I had said by the least shadow of a flicker I yet somehow felt, it was yet somehow conveyed to me, that perhaps in French one doesn't perspire, or if one does one doesn't talk about it. Not if one is a lady. Not if one is Madame. Not, to ascend still further the scale of my self-respect enforcing attributes, if one is that dignified object the *patrone.*

I find it difficult to be dignified. When I try, I overdo it. Always my dignity is either over or under done, but its chief condition is that of being under done. Antoine, however, very kindly helps me up to the position he has decided I ought to fill, by his own unalterable calm. I have never seen him smile. I don't believe he could without cracking, of so unruffled a glassiness is his countenance.

Once, before the war—everything I have done that has been cheerful and undesirable was before the war; I've been nothing but exemplary and wretched since—I was undignified. We dressed up; and on the advice of my friends—I now see that it was bad advice—I allowed myself to be dressed as a devil; I, the *patrone*; I, Madame. It was true I was only a little devil, quite one of the minor ones, what the Germans would call a *Hausteufelchen*; but a devil I was. And going upstairs again unexpectedly, to fetch my tail which had been forgotten, I saw at the very end of the long passage, down which I had to go, Antoine collecting the day's boots.

He stood aside and waited. I couldn't go back, because that would have looked as though I were doing something I knew I oughtn't to. Therefore I proceeded.

The passage was long and well lit. Down the whole of it I had to go, while Antoine at the end stood and waited. I tried to advance with dignity. I tried to hope he wouldn't recognise me. I tried to feel sure he wouldn't. How could he? I was quite black, except for a wig that looked like orange-coloured flames. But when I got to the doors at the end it was the one to my bedroom that Antoine threw open, and past him I had to march while he stood gravely aside. And strangely enough, what I remember feeling most acutely was a quite particular humiliation and shame that I hadn't got my tail on.

'*C'est que j'ai oublié ma queue....*' I found myself stammering, with a look of agonised deprecation and apology at him.

And even then Antoine wasn't surprised.

Well, where was I? Oh yes—at the *transpiration*. Antoine let it pass over him, as I have said, without a ruffle, and drew my attention to the chickens who would have to be fed and the cow who would have to be milked. Perhaps the cow might be milked on his return, but the chickens—

Antoine was softening.

I said quickly that all he had to do would be to put the chickens' food ready and I would administer it, and as for the cow, why not let her have a rest for once, why not let her for once not be robbed of what was after all her own?

And to cut the conversation short, and determined that my birthday should not pass without somebody getting a present, I ran upstairs and fetched down a twenty-franc note and pressed it into Antoine's hand and said breathlessly in a long and voluble sentence that began with *Voilà*, but didn't keep it up at that level, that the twenty francs were for his expenses for himself and Mrs. Antoine down in the valley, and that I hoped they would enjoy themselves, and would he remember me very kindly to his *maman*, to whom he would no doubt pay a little visit during the course of what I trusted would be a long, crowded, and agreeable day.

They went off ultimately, but with reluctance. Completely undignified, I stood on the low wall of the terrace and waved to them as they turned the corner at the bottom of the path.

'*Mille félicitations!*' I cried, anxious that somebody should be wished happiness on my birthday.

'If I *am* going to have a lonely birthday it shall be *thoroughly* lonely,' I said grimly to myself as, urged entirely by my volition, the Antoines disappeared and left me to the solitary house.

I decided to begin my day's work by making my bed, and went upstairs full of resolution.

Mrs. Antoine, however, had done that; no doubt while I was arguing with Antoine.

The next thing, then, I reflected, was to tidy away breakfast, so I came downstairs again, full of more resolution.

Mrs. Antoine, however, had done that too; no doubt while I was still arguing with Antoine.

Well then, oughtn't I to begin to do something with potatoes? With a view to the dinner-hour? Put them on, or something? I was sure the putting on of potatoes would make me perspire. I longed to start my *transpiration* in case by any chance, if I stayed too long inactive and cool, I should notice how very silent and empty....

I hurried into the kitchen, a dear little place of white tiles and copper saucepans, and found pots simmering gently on the stove: potatoes in one, and in the other bits of something that well might be chicken. Also, on a tray was the rest of everything needed for my dinner. All I would have to do would be to eat it.

Baulked, but still full of resolution, I set out in search of the lawn-mower. It couldn't be far away, because nothing is able to be anything but close on my narrow ledge of rock.

Mou-Mou, sitting on his haunches in the shade at the back of the house, watched me with interest as I tried to open the sorts of outside doors that looked as if they shut in lawn-mowers.

They were all locked.

The magnificent Mou-Mou, who manages to imitate Antoine's trick of not being surprised, though he hasn't yet quite caught his air of absence of curiosity, got up after the first door and lounged after me as I tried the others. He could do this because, though tied up, Antoine has ingeniously provided for his exercise, and at the same time for the circumvention of burglars, by fixing an iron bar the whole length of the wall behind the house and fastening Mou-Mou's chain to it by a loose ring. So that he can run along it whenever he feels inclined; and a burglar, having noted the kennel at the east end of this wall and Mou-Mou sitting chained up in front of it, would find, on preparing to attack the house at its west and apparently dogless end, that the dog was nevertheless there before him. A rattle and a slide, and there would be Mou-Mou. Very *morale*-shaking. Very freezing in its unexpectedness to the burglar's blood, and paralysing to his will to sin. Thus Antoine, thinking of everything, had calculated. There hasn't ever been a burglar, but, as he said of his possible suppurating wounds, '*Il ne faut pas attendre qu'on les a pour se procurer le remède.*'

Mou-Mou accordingly came with me as I went up and down the back of the house trying the range of outside doors. I think he thought at last it was a game, for as each door wouldn't open and I paused a moment thwarted, he gave a loud double bark, as one who should in the Psalms, after each verse, say *Selah*.

Antoine had locked up the lawn-mower. The mowing was to be put off till to-morrow rather than that Madame in the heat should mow. I appreciated the kindness of his intentions, but for all that was much vexed by being baulked. On my birthday too. Baulked of the one thing I really wanted, *la transpiration*. It didn't seem much to ask on my birthday, I who used, without so much as lifting a finger, to acquire on such occasions quite other beads.

Undecided, I stood looking round the tidy yard for something I could be active over, and Mou-Mou sat upright on his huge haunches watching me. He is so big that in this position our heads are on a level. He took advantage of this by presently raising his tongue—it was already out, hanging in the heat—as I still didn't move or say anything, and giving my face an enormous lick. So then I went away, for I didn't like that. Besides, I had thought of something.

In the flower-border along the terrace would be weeds. Flower-borders always have weeds, and weeding is arduous. Also, all one wants for weeding are one's own ten fingers, and Antoine couldn't prevent my using those. So that was what I would do—bend down and tear up weeds, and in this way forget the extraordinary sunlit, gaping, empty little house....

So great, however, had been the unflagging diligence of Antoine, and also perhaps so poor and barren the soil, that after half an hour's search I had only found three weeds, and even those I couldn't be sure about, and didn't know for certain but what I might be pulling up some precious bit of alpine flora put in on purpose and cherished by Antoine. All I really knew was that what I tore up wasn't irises, and wasn't delphiniums, and wasn't pansies; so that, I argued, it must be weeds. Anyhow, I pulled three alien objects out, and laid them in a neat row to show Antoine. Then I sat down and rested.

The search for them had made me hot, but that of course wouldn't last. It was ages before I need go and feed the chickens. I sat on the terrace wall wondering what I could do next. It was a pity that the Antoines were so admirable. One could overdo virtue. A little less

18

zeal, the least judicious neglect on their part, and I would have found something useful to do.

The place was quite extraordinarily silent. There wasn't a sound. Even Mou-Mou round at the back, languid in the heat, didn't move. The immense light beat on the varnished wooden face of the house and on the shut shutters of all the unused rooms. Those rooms have been shut like that for five years. The shutters are blistered with the fierce sun of five summers, and the no less fierce sun of five winters. Their colour, once a lively, swaggering blue, has faded to a dull grey: I sat staring up at them. Suppose they were suddenly to be opened from inside, and faces that used to live in them looked out?

A faint shudder trickled along my spine.

Well, but wouldn't I be glad really? Wouldn't they be the dearest ghosts? That room at the end, for instance, so tightly shut up now, that was where my brother used to sleep when he came out for his holidays. Wouldn't I love to see him look out at me? How gaily he used to arrive,—in such spirits because he had got rid of work for a bit, and for a series of divine weeks was going to stretch himself in the sun! The first thing he always did when he got up to his room was to hurry out on to its little balcony to see if the heavenly view of the valley towards the east with the chain of snow mountains across the end were still as heavenly as he remembered it; and I could see him with his head thrown back, breathing deep breaths of the lovely air, adoring it, radiant with delight to have got back to it, calling down to me to come quick and look, for it could never have been so beautiful as at that moment and could never possibly be so beautiful again.

I loved him very much. I don't believe anybody ever had so dear a brother. He was so quick to appreciate and understand, so slow to anger, so clear of brain and gentle of heart. Of course he was killed. Such people always are, if there is any killing going on anywhere. He volunteered at the very beginning of the war, and though his fragility saved him for a long time he was at last swept in. That was in March 1918. He was killed the first week. I loved him very much, and he loved me. He called me sweet names, and forgave me all my trespasses.

And in the next room to that—oh well, I'm not going to dig out every ghost. I can't really write about some of them, the pain hurts too much. I've not been into any of the shut rooms since I came back. I couldn't bear it. Here out of doors I can take a larger view, not mind going to the places of memories; but I know those rooms will have been kept as carefully unchanged by Antoine as I found mine. I daren't even think of them. I had to get up off the wall and come away from staring up at those shutters, for suddenly I found myself right on the very edge of the dreadful pit I'm always so afraid of tumbling into—the great, black, cold, empty pit of horror, of realisation....

That's why I've been writing all this, just so as not to think....

Bedtime.

I must put down what happened after that. I ought to be in bed, but I must put down how my birthday ended.

Well, there I was sitting, trying by writing to defend myself against the creeping fear of the silence round me and the awareness of those shut rooms up stairs, when Mou-Mou barked. He barked suddenly and furiously; and the long screech of his chain showed that he was rushing along the wall to the other side of the house.

Instantly my thoughts became wholesome. I jumped up. Here was the burglar at last. I flew round to greet him. Anything was better than those shutters, and that hot, sunlit silence.

Between my departure from the terrace and my arrival at the other side of the house I had had time, so quickly did my restored mind work, to settle that whoever it was, burglar or not, I was going to make friends. If it really were a burglar I would adopt the line the bishop took towards Jean Valjean, and save him from the sin of theft by making him a present of everything he wished to take,—conduct which perhaps might save me as well, supposing he was the kind of burglar who would want to strangle opposition. Also, burglar or no burglar, I would ask him to dinner; compel him, in fact, to come in and share my birthday chicken.

What I saw when I got round, standing just out of reach of the leaping Mou-Mou on the top of the avalanche wall, looking down at him with patience rather than timidity,

19

holding their black skirts back in case an extra leap of his should reach them, were two women. Strangers, not natives. Perhaps widows. But anyhow people who had been bereaved.

I immediately begged them to come in. The relief and refreshment of seeing them! Two human beings of obvious respectability, warm flesh and blood persons, not burglars, not ghosts, not even of the sex one associates with depredation,—just decent, alive women, complete in every detail, even to each carrying an umbrella. They might have been standing on the curb in Oxford Street waiting to hail an omnibus, so complete were they, so prepared in their clothes to face the world. Button boots, umbrella,—I hadn't seen an umbrella since I got here. What you usually take for a walk on the mountains is a stout stick with an iron point to it; but after all, why shouldn't you take an umbrella? Then if it rains you can put it up, and if the sun is unbearable you can put it up too, and it too has a metal tip to it which you can dig into the ground if you begin to slide down precipices.

'*Bon jour*,' I said eagerly, looking up at these black silhouettes against the sky. '*Je vous prie de venir me voir.*'

They stared at me, still holding back their skirts from the leaping dog.

Perhaps they were Italians. I am close to Italy, and Italian women usually dress in black.

I know some Italian words, and I know the one you say when you want somebody to come in, so I tried that.

'*Avanti*,' I said breathlessly.

They didn't. They still just stood and stared.

They couldn't be English I thought, because underneath their black skirts I could see white cotton petticoats with embroidery on them, the kind that England has shed these fifty years, and that is only now to be found in remote and religious parts of abroad, like the more fervent portions of Lutheran Germany. Could they be Germans? The thought distracted me. How could I ask two Germans in? How could I sit at meat with people whose male relations had so recently been killing mine? Or been killed by them, perhaps, judging from their black clothes. Anyhow there was blood between us. But how could I resist asking them in, when if I didn't there would be hours and hours of intolerable silence and solitude for me, till evening brought those Antoines back who never ought to have been let go? On my birthday, too.

I know some German words—it is wonderful what a lot of languages I seem to know some words in—so I threw one up at them between two of Mou-Mou's barks.

'*Deutsch?*' I inquired.

They ignored it.

'That's all my languages,' I then said in despair.

The only thing left that I might still try on them was to talk on my fingers, which I can a little; but if they didn't happen, I reflected, to be deaf and dumb perhaps they wouldn't like that. So I just looked at them despairingly, and spread out my hands and drew my shoulders to my ears as Mrs. Antoine does when she is conveying to me that the butter has come to an end.

Whereupon the elder of the two—neither was young, but one was less young—the elder of the two informed me in calm English that they had lost their way, and she asked me to direct them and also to tell the dog not to make quite so much noise, in order that they might clearly understand what I said. 'He is a fine fellow,' she said, 'but we should be glad if he would make less noise.'

The younger one said nothing, but smiled at me. She was pleasant-looking, this one, flushed and nicely moist from walking in the heat. The other one was more rocky; considering the weather, and the angle of the slope they had either come up or down, she seemed quite unnaturally arid.

I seized Mou-Mou by the collar, and ran him along to his kennel.

'You stay there and be good,' I said to him, though I know he doesn't understand a word of English. 'He won't hurt you,' I assured the strangers, going back to them.

'Ah,' said the elder of the two; and added, 'I used to say that to people about *my* dog.'

They still stood motionless, holding their skirts, the younger one smiling at me.

20

'Won't you come down?' I said. 'Come in and rest a little? I can tell you better about your road if you'll come in. Look—you go along that path there, and it brings you round to the front door.'

'Will the dog be at the front door?' asked the elder.

'Oh no—besides, he wouldn't hurt a fly.'

'Ah,' said the elder eyeing Mou-Mou sideways, who, from his kennel, eyed her, 'I used to say that to people about *my* dog.'

The younger one stood smiling at me. They neither of them moved.

'I'll come up and bring you down,' I said, hurrying round to the path that leads from the terrace on to the slope.

When they saw that this path did indeed take them away from Mou-Mou they came with me.

Directly they moved he made a rush along his bar, but arrived too late and could only leap up and down barking.

'That's just high spirits,' I said. 'He is really most goodnatured and affectionate.'

'Ah,' said the elder, 'I used to say that to people—'

'Mind those loose stones,' I interrupted; and I helped each one down the last crumbly bit on to the terrace

They both had black kid gloves on. More than ever, as I felt these warm gloves press my hand, was I sure that what they really wanted was an omnibus along Oxford Street.

Once on the level and out of sight of Mou-Mou, they walked with an air of self-respect. Especially the elder. The younger, though she had it too, seemed rather to be following an example than originating an attitude. Perhaps they were related to a Lord Mayor, I thought. Or a rector. But a Lord Mayor would be more likely to be the cause of that air of glowing private background to life.

They had been up the mountain, the elder told me, trying to find somewhere cool to stay in, for the valley this weather was unendurable. They used to know this district years ago, and recollected a pension right up in the highest village, and after great exertions and rising early that morning they had reached it only to find that it had become a resort for consumptives. With no provision for the needs of the passing tourist; with no desire, in fact, in any way to minister to them. If it hadn't been for me, she said, as they sat on the cool side of the house drinking lemonade and eating biscuits, if it hadn't been for me and what she described with obvious gratitude—she couldn't guess my joy at seeing them both!—as my kindness, they would have had somehow to clamber down foodless by wrong roads, seeing that they had lost the right one, to the valley again, and in what state they would have re-entered that scorching and terrible place she didn't like to think. Tired as they were. Disappointed, and distressingly hot. How very pleasant it was up here. What a truly delightful spot. Such air. Such a view. And how agreeable and unexpected to come across one of one's own country-women.

To all this the younger in silence smiled agreement.

They had been so long abroad, continued the elder, that they felt greatly fatigued by foreigners, who were so very prevalent. In their pension there were nothing but foreigners and flies. The house wasn't by any chance—no, of course it couldn't be, but it wasn't by any chance—her voice had a sudden note of hope in it—a pension?

I shook my head and laughed at that, and said it wasn't. The younger one smiled at me.

Ah no—of course not, continued the elder, her voice fading again. And she didn't suppose I could tell them of any pension anywhere about, where they could get taken in while this great heat lasted? Really the valley was most terribly airless. The best hotel, which had, she knew, some cool rooms, was beyond their means, so they were staying in one of the small ones, and the flies worried them. Apparently I had no flies up here. And what wonderful air. At night, no doubt, it was quite cool. The nights in the valley were most trying. It was difficult to sleep.

I asked them to stay to lunch. They accepted gratefully. When I took them to my room to wash their hands they sighed with pleasure at its shadiness and quiet. They thought the inside of the house delightfully roomy, and more spacious, said the elder, while the younger one smiled agreement, than one would have expected from its outside. I left them, sunk with sighs of satisfaction, on the sofa in the hall, their black toques and gloves on a chair beside them, gazing at the view through the open front door while I went to see how the potatoes were getting on.

We lunched presently in the shade just outside the house, and the strange ladies continued to be most grateful, the elder voicing their gratitude, the younger smiling agreement. If it was possible to like one more than the other, seeing with what enthusiasm I liked them both, I liked the younger because she smiled. I love people who smile. It does usually mean sweet pleasantness somewhere.

After lunch, while I cleared away, having refused their polite offers of help,—for they now realised I was alone in the house, on which, however, though it must have surprised them they made no comment,—they went indoors to the sofa again, whose soft cushions seemed particularly attractive to them; and when I came back the last time for the breadcrumbs and tablecloth, I found they had both fallen asleep, the elder one with her handkerchief over her face.

Poor things. How tired they were. How glad I was that they should be resting and getting cool. A little sleep would do them both good.

I crept past them on tiptoe with my final armful, and was careful to move about in the kitchen very quietly. It hadn't been my intention, with guests to lunch, to wash up and put away, but rather to sit with them and talk. Not having talked for so long it seemed a godsend, a particularly welcome birthday present, suddenly to have two English people drop in on me from the skies. Up to this moment I had been busy, first getting lemonade to slake their thirst and then lunch to appease their hunger, and the spare time in between these activities had been filled with the expression of their gratitude by the elder and her expatiations on the house and what she called the grounds; but I had looked forward to about an hour's real talk after lunch, before they would begin to want to start on their long downward journey to their pension,—talk in which, without being specially brilliant any of us, for you only had to look at us to see we wouldn't be specially that, we yet might at least tell each other amusing things about, say, Lord Mayors. It is true I don't know any Lord Mayors, though I do know somebody whose brother married the daughter of one; but if they could produce a Lord Mayor out of up their sleeve, as I suspected, I could counter him with a dean. Not quite so showy, perhaps, but more permanent. And I did want to talk. I have been silent so long that I felt I could talk about almost anything.

Well, as they were having a little nap, poor things, I would tidy up the kitchen meanwhile, and by the time that was done they would be refreshed and ready for half an hour's agreeable interchange of gossip.

Every now and then during this tidying I peeped into the hall in case they were awake, but they seemed if anything to be sounder asleep each time. The younger one, her flushed face half buried in a cushion, her fair hair a little ruffled, had a pathetic look of almost infantile helplessness; the elder, discreetly veiled by her handkerchief, slept more stiffly, with less abandonment and more determination. Poor things. How glad I was they should in this way gather strength for the long, difficult scramble down the mountain; but also presently I began to wish they would wake up.

I finished what I had to do in the kitchen, and came back into the hall. They had been sleeping now nearly half an hour. I stood about uncertainly. Poor things, they must be dreadfully tired to sleep like that. I hardly liked to look at them, they were so defenceless, and I picked up a book and tried to read; but I couldn't stop my eyes from wandering over the top of it to the sofa every few minutes, and always I saw the same picture of profound repose.

Presently I put down the book, and wandered out on to the terrace and gazed awhile at the view. That, too, seemed wrapped in afternoon slumber. After a bit I wandered round the house to Mou-Mou. He, too, was asleep. Then I came back to the front door and glanced in at my guests. Still no change. Then I fetched some cigarettes, not moving this time quite so carefully, and going out again sat on the low terrace-wall at a point from which I could see straight on to the sofa and notice any movement that might take place.

I never smoke except when bored, and as I am never bored I never smoke. But this afternoon it was just that unmanageable sort of moment come upon me, that kind of situation I don't know how to deal with, which does bore me. I sat on the wall and smoked three cigarettes, and the peace on the sofa remained complete. What ought one to do? What did one do, faced by obstinately sleeping guests? Impossible deliberately to wake them up. Yet I was sure—they had now been asleep nearly an hour—that when they did wake up, polite as they were, they would be upset by discovering that they had slept. Besides, the afternoon was getting on. They had a long way to go. If only Mou-Mou would wake up and bark.... But there wasn't a sound. The hot afternoon brooded over the mountains in breathless silence.

Again I went round to the back of the house, and pausing behind the last corner so as to make what I did next more alarming, suddenly jumped out at Mou Mou.

The horribly intelligent dog didn't bother to open more than an eye, and that one he immediately shut again.

Disgusted with him, I returned to my seat on the wall and smoked another cigarette. The picture on the sofa was the same: perfect peace. Oh well, poor things—but I did want to talk. And after all it was my birthday.

When I had finished the cigarette I thought a moment, my face in my hands. A person of tact—ah, but I have no tact; it has been my undoing on the cardinal occasions of life that I have none. Well, but suppose I *were* a person of tact—what would I do? Instantly the answer flashed into my brain: Knock, by accident, against a table.

So I did. I got up quickly and crossed into the hall and knocked against a table, at first with gentleness, and then as there was no result with greater vigour.

My elder guest behind the handkerchief continued to draw deep regular breaths, but to my joy the younger one stirred and opened her eyes.

'Oh, I do *hope* I didn't wake you?' I exclaimed, taking an eager step towards the sofa.

She looked at me vaguely, and fell asleep again.

I went back on to the terrace and lit another cigarette. That was five. I haven't smoked so much before in one day in my life ever. I felt quite fast. And on my birthday too. By the time I had finished it there was a look about the shadows on the grass that suggested tea. Even if it were a little early the noise of the teacups might help to wake up my guests, and I felt that a call to tea would be a delicate and hospitable way of doing it.

I didn't go through the hall on tiptoe this time, but walked naturally; and I opened the door into the kitchen rather noisily. Then I looked round at the sofa to see the effect. There wasn't any.

Presently tea was ready, out on the table where we had lunched. At least six times I had been backwards and forwards through the hall, the last twice carrying things that rattled and that I encouraged to rattle. But on the sofa the strangers slept peacefully on.

There was nothing for it now but to touch them. Short of that, I didn't think that anything would wake them. But I don't like touching guests; I mean, in between whiles. I have never done it. Especially not when they weren't looking. And still more especially not when they were complete strangers.

Therefore I approached the sofa with reluctance, and stood uncertain in front of it. Poor things, they really were most completely asleep. It seemed a pity to interrupt. Well, but they had had a nice rest; they had slept soundly now for two hours. And the tea would be cold if I didn't wake them up, and besides, how were they going to get home if they didn't start soon? Still, I don't like touching guests. Especially strange guests....

Manifestly, however, there was nothing else to be done, so I bent over the younger one—the other one was too awe-inspiring with her handkerchief over her face—and gingerly put my hand on her shoulder.

Nothing happened.

I put it on again, with a slightly increased emphasis.

She didn't open her eyes, but to my embarrassment laid her cheek on it affectionately and murmured something that sounded astonishingly like Siegfried.

I know about Siegfried, because of going to the opera. He was a German. He still is, in the form of Siegfried Wagner, and I daresay of others; and once somebody told me that

23

when Germans wished to indulge their disrespect for the Kaiser freely—he was not at that time yet an ex-Kaiser—without being run in for *lèse majesté*, they loudly and openly abused him under the name of Siegfried Meyer, whose initials, S.M., also represent *Seine Majestät*; by which simple methods everybody was able to be pleased and nobody was able to be hurt. So that when my sleeping guest murmured Siegfried, I couldn't but conclude she was dreaming of a German; and when at the same time she laid her cheek on my hand, I was forced to realise that she was dreaming of him affectionately. Which astonished me.

Imbued with patriotism—the accumulated patriotism of weeks spent out of England—I felt that this English lady should instantly be roused from a dream that did her no credit. She herself, I felt sure, would be the first to deplore such a dream. So I drew my hand away from beneath her cheek—even by mistake I didn't like it to be thought the hand of somebody called Siegfried and, stooping down, said quite loud and distinctly in her ear, 'Won't you come to tea?'

This, at last, did wake her. She sat up with a start, and looked at me for a moment in surprise.

'Oh,' she said, confused, 'have I been asleep?'

'I'm very glad you have,' I said, smiling at her, for she was already again smiling at me. 'Your climb this morning was enough to kill you.'

'Oh, but,' she murmured, getting up quickly and straightening her hair, 'how dreadful to come to your house and go to sleep—'

And she turned to the elder one, and again astonished me by, with one swift movement, twitching the handkerchief off her face and saying exactly as one says when playing the face-and-handkerchief game with one's baby, 'Peep bo.' Then she turned back to me and smiled and said nothing more, for I suppose she knew the elder one, roused thus competently, would now do all the talking; as indeed she did, being as I feared greatly upset and horrified when she found she had not only been asleep but been it for two hours.

We had tea; and all the while, while the elder one talked of the trouble she was afraid she had given, and the shame she felt that they should have slept, and their gratitude for what she called my prolonged and patient hospitality, I was wondering about the other. Whenever she caught my pensive and inquiring eye she smiled at me. She had very sweet eyes, grey ones, gentle and intelligent, and when she smiled an agreeable dimple appeared. Bringing my Paley's *Evidences* and Sherlock Holmes' side to bear on her, I reasoned that my younger guest was, or had been, a mother,—this because of the practised way she had twitched the handkerchief off and said Peep bo; that she was either a widow, or hadn't seen her husband for some time,—this because of the real affection with which, in her sleep she had laid her cheek on my hand; and that she liked music and often went to the opera.

After tea the elder got up stiffly—she had walked much too far already, and was clearly unfit to go all that long way more—and said, if I would direct them, they must now set out for the valley.

The younger one put on her toque obediently at this, and helped the elder one to pin hers on straight. It was now five o'clock, and if they didn't once lose their way they would be at their hotel by half-past seven; in time, said the elder, for the end of *table-d'hôte,* a meal much interfered with by the very numerous flies. But if they did go wrong at any point it would be much later, probably dark.

I asked them to stay.

To stay? The elder, engaged in buttoning her tight kid gloves, said it was most kind of me, but they couldn't possibly stay any longer. It was far too late already, owing to their so unfortunately having gone to sleep—

'I mean stay the night,' I said; and explained that it would be doing me a kindness, and because of that they must please overlook anything in such an invitation that might appear unconventional, for certainly if they did set out I should lie awake all night thinking of them lost somewhere among the precipices, or perhaps fallen over one, and how much better to go down comfortably in daylight, and I could lend them everything they wanted, including a great many new toothbrushes I found here,—in short, I not only invited, I pressed; growing more eager by the sheer gathering momentum of my speech.

All day, while the elder talked and I listened, I had secretly felt uneasy. Here was I, one woman in a house arranged for family gatherings, while they for want of rooms were forced to swelter in the valley. Gradually, as I listened, my uneasiness increased. Presently I began to feel guilty. And at last, as I watched them sleeping in such exhaustion on the sofa, I felt at the bottom of my heart somehow responsible. But I don't know, of course, that it is wise to invite strangers to stay with one.

They accepted gratefully. The moment the elder understood what it was that my eager words were pressing on her, she drew the pins out of her toque and laid it on the chair again; and so did the other one, smiling at me.

When the Antoines came home I went out to meet them. By that time my guests were shut up in their bedrooms with new toothbrushes. They had gone up very early, both of them so stiff that they could hardly walk. Till they did go up, what moments I had been able to spare from my hasty preparations for their comfort had been filled entirely, as earlier in the day, by the elder one's gratitude; there had still been no chance of real talk.

'*J'ai des visites*,' I said to the Antoines, going out to meet them when, through the silence of the evening, I heard their steps coming up the path.

Antoine wasn't surprised. He just said, '*Ça sera comme autrefois*,' and began to shut the shutters.

But I am. I can't go to bed, I'm so much surprised. I've been sitting up here scribbling when I ought to have been in bed long ago. Who would have thought that the day that began so emptily would end with two of my rooms full,—each containing a widow? For they are widows, they told me: widows who have lost their husbands by peaceful methods, nothing to do with the war. Their names are Mrs. Barnes and Mrs. Jewks,—at least that is what the younger one's sounded like; I don't know if I have spelt it right. They come from Dulwich. I think the elder one had a slight misgiving at the last, and seemed to remember what was due to the Lord Mayor, when she found herself going to bed in a strange house belonging to somebody of whom she knew nothing; for she remarked a little doubtfully, and with rather a defensive eye fixed on me, that the war had broken down many barriers, and that people did things now that they wouldn't have dreamed of doing five years ago.

The other one didn't say nothing, but actually kissed me. I hope she wasn't again mistaking me for Siegfried.

August 15th

My guests have gone again, but only to fetch their things and pay their hotel bill, and then they are coming back to stay with me till it is a little cooler. They are coming back to-morrow, not to-day. They are entangled in some arrangement with their pension that makes it difficult for them to leave at once.

Mrs. Barnes appeared at breakfast with any misgivings she may have had last night gone, for when I suggested they should spend this hot weather up here she immediately accepted. I hadn't slept for thinking of them. How could I possibly not ask them to stay, seeing their discomfort and my roominess? Towards morning it was finally clear to me that it wasn't possible: I would ask them. Though, remembering the look in Mrs. Barnes's eye the last thing last night, I couldn't be sure she would accept. She might want to find out about me first, after the cautious and hampering way of women,—oh, I wish women wouldn't always be so cautious, but simply get on with their friendships! She might first want assurances that there was some good reason for my being here all by myself. Alas, there isn't a good reason; there is only a bad one. But, fortunately, to be alone is generally regarded as respectable, in spite of what Seneca says a philosopher said to a young man he saw walking by himself: 'Have a care,' said he, 'of lewd company.'

However, I don't suppose Mrs. Barnes knew about Seneca. Anyhow she didn't hesitate. She accepted at once, and said that under these circumstances it was certainly due to me to tell me a little about themselves.

At this I got my dean ready to meet the Lord Mayor, but after all I was told nothing more than that my guests are sisters; for at this point, very soon arrived at, the younger one, Mrs. Jewks, who had slipped away on our getting up from breakfast, reappeared with the toques and gloves, and said she thought they had better start before it got any hotter.

So they went, and the long day here has been most beautiful—so peaceful, so quiet, with the delicate mountains like opals against the afternoon sky, and the shadows lengthening along the valley.

I don't feel to-day as I did yesterday, that I want to talk. To-day I am content with things exactly as they are: the sun, the silence, the caresses of the funny little white kitten with the smudge of black round its left eye that makes it look as though it must be somebody's wife, and the pleasant knowledge that my new friends are coming back again.

I think that knowledge makes to-day more precious. It is the last day for some time, for at least a week judging from the look of the blazing sky, of what I see now that they are ending have been wonderful days. Up the ladder of these days I have climbed slowly away from the blackness at the bottom. It has been like finding some steps under water just as one was drowning, and crawling up them to air and light. But now that I have got at least most of myself back to air and light, and feel hopeful of not slipping down again, it is surely time to arise, shake myself, and begin to do something active and fruitful. And behold, just as I realise this, just as I realise that I am, so to speak, ripe for fruit-bearing, there appear on the scene Mrs. Barnes and Mrs. Jewks, as it were the midwives of Providence.

Well, that shall be to-morrow. Meanwhile there is still to-day, and each one of its quiet hours seems very precious. I wonder what my new friends like to read. Suppose—I was going to say suppose it is *The Rosary*; but I won't suppose that, for when it comes to supposing, why not suppose something that isn't *The Rosary*? Why not, for instance, suppose they like *Eminent Victorians*, and that we three are going to sit of an evening delicately tickling each other with quotations from it, and gently squirming in our seats for pleasure? It is just as easy to suppose that as to suppose anything else, and as I'm not yet acquainted with these ladies' tastes one supposition is as likely to be right as another.

I don't know, though—I forgot their petticoats. I can't believe any friends of Mr. Lytton Strachey wear that kind of petticoat, eminently Victorian even though it be; and although he wouldn't, of course, have direct ocular proof that they did unless he had stood with me yesterday at the bottom of that wall while they on the top held up their skirts, still what one has on underneath does somehow ooze through into one's behaviour. I know once, when impelled by a heat wave in America to cast aside the undergarments of a candid mind and buy and put on pink chiffon, the pink chiffon instantly got through all my clothes into my conduct, which became curiously dashing. Anybody can tell what a woman has got on underneath by merely watching her behaviour. I have known just the consciousness of silk stockings, worn by one accustomed only to wool, produce dictatorialness where all before had been submission.

August 19th

I haven't written for three days because I have been so busy settling down to my guests.

They call each other Kitty and Dolly. They explained that these were inevitably their names because they were born, one fifty, the other forty years ago. I inquired why this was inevitable, and they drew my attention to fashions in names, asserting that people's ages could generally be guessed by their Christian names. If, they said, their birth had taken place ten years earlier they would have been Ethel and Maud; if ten years later they would have been Muriel and Gladys; and if twenty years only ago they had no doubt but what they would have been Elizabeth and Pamela. It is always Mrs. Barnes who talks; but the effect is as though they together were telling me things, because of the way Mrs. Jewks smiles,—I conclude in agreement.

'Our dear parents, both long since dead,' said Mrs. Barnes, adjusting her eyeglasses more comfortably on her nose, 'didn't seem to remember that we would ever grow old, for we weren't even christened Katharine and Dorothy, to which we might have reverted when we ceased being girls, but we were Kitty and Dolly from the very beginning, and actually in that condition came away from the font.'

'I like being Dolly,' murmured Mrs. Jewks.

Mrs. Barnes looked at her with what I thought was a slight uneasiness, and rebuked her. 'You shouldn't,' she said. 'After thirty-nine no woman should willingly be Dolly.'

'I still feel exactly *like* Dolly,' murmured Mrs. Jewks.

'It's a misfortune,' said Mrs. Barnes, shaking her head. 'To be called Dolly after a certain age is bad enough, but it is far worse to feel like it. What I think of,' she said, turning to me, 'is when we are really old,—in bath chairs, unable to walk, and no doubt being spoon fed, and yet obliged to continue to be called by these names. It will rob us of dignity.'

'I don't think I'll mind,' murmured Mrs. Jewks. 'I shall still feel exactly *like* Dolly.'

Mrs. Barnes looked at her, again I thought with uneasiness—with, really, an air of rather anxious responsibility.

And afterwards, when her sister had gone indoors for something, she expounded a theory she said she held, the soundness of which had often been proved to her by events, that names had much influence on behaviour.

'Not half as much,' I thought (but didn't say), 'as underclothes.' And indeed I have for years been acquainted with somebody called Trixy, who for steady gloom and heaviness of spirit would be hard to equal. Also I know an Isolda; a most respectable married woman, of a sprightly humour and much nimbleness in dodging big emotions.

'Dolly,' said Mrs. Barnes, 'has never, I am sorry to say, shared my opinion. If she had, many things in her life would have been different, for then she would have been on her guard as I have been. I am glad to say there is nothing I have ever done since I ceased to be a child that has been even remotely compatible with being called Kitty.'

I said I thought that was a great deal to be able to say. It suggested, I said, quite an unusually blameless past. Through my brain ran for an instant the vision of that devil who, seeking his tail, met Antoine in the passage. I blushed. Fortunately Mrs. Barnes didn't notice.

'What did Dol—what did Mrs. Jewks do,' I said, 'that you think was the direct result of her Christian name? Don't tell me if my question is indiscreet, which I daresay it is, because I know I often am, but your theory interests me.'

Mrs. Barnes hesitated a moment. She was, I think, turning over in her mind whether she would give herself the relief of complete unreserve, or continue for a few more days to skim round on the outskirts of confidences. This was yesterday. After all, she had only been with me two days.

She considered awhile, then decided that two days wasn't long enough, so only said: 'My sister is sometimes a little rash,—or perhaps I should say has been. But the effects of rashness are felt for a long time; usually for the rest of one's life.'

'Yes,' I agreed; and thought ruefully of some of my own.

This, however, only made me if anything more inquisitive as to the exact nature and quality of Dolly's resemblance to her name. We all, I suppose (except Mrs. Barnes, who I am sure hasn't), have been rash, and if we could induce ourselves to be frank much innocent amusement might be got by comparing the results of our rashnesses. But Mrs. Barnes was unable at the moment to induce herself to be frank, and she returned to the subject she has already treated very fully since her arrival, the wonderful bracing air up here and her great and grateful appreciation of it.

To-day is Tuesday; and on Saturday evening,—the day they arrived back again, complete with their luggage, which came up in a cart round by the endless zigzags of the road while they with their peculiar dauntlessness took the steep short cuts,—we had what might be called an exchange of cards. Mrs. Barnes told me what she thought fit for me to know about her late husband, and I responded by telling her and her sister what I thought fit for them to know of my uncle the Dean.

There is such a lot of him that is fit to know that it took some time. He was a great convenience. How glad I am I've got him. A dean, after all, is of an impressive respectability as a relation. His apron covers a multitude of family shortcomings. You can hold him up to the light, and turn him round, and view him from every angle, and there is nothing about him that doesn't bear inspection. All my relations aren't like that. One at least, though he denies it, wasn't even born in wedlock. We're not sure about the others, but we're quite sure about this one, that he wasn't born altogether as he ought to have been. Except for his obstinacy in denial he is a very attractive person. My uncle can't be got to see that he exists. This makes him not able to like my uncle.

I didn't go beyond the Dean on Saturday night, for he had a most satisfying effect on my new friends. Mrs. Barnes evidently thinks highly of deans, and Mrs. Jewks, though she said nothing, smiled very pleasantly while I held him up to view. No Lord Mayor was produced on their side. I begin to think there isn't one. I begin to think their self-respect is simply due to the consciousness that they are British. Not that Mrs. Jewks says anything about it, but she smiles while Mrs. Barnes talks on immensely patriotic lines. I gather they haven't been in England for some time, so that naturally their affection for their country has been fanned into a great glow. I know all about that sort of glow. I have had it each time I've been out of England.

August 20th.

Mrs. Barnes elaborated the story of him she speaks of always as Mr. Barnes to-day.

He was, she said, a business man, and went to the city every day, where he did things with hides: dried skins, I understood, that he bought and resold. And though Mr. Barnes drew his sustenance from these hides with what seemed to Mrs. Barnes great ease and abundance while he was alive, after his death it was found that, through no fault of his own but rather, she suggested, to his credit, he had for some time past been living on his capital. This capital came to an end almost simultaneously with Mr. Barnes, and all that was left for Mrs. Barnes to live on was the house at Dulwich, handsomely furnished, it was true, with everything of the best; for Mr. Barnes had disliked what Mrs. Barnes called fandangles, and was all for mahogany and keeping a good table. But you can't live on mahogany, said Mrs. Barnes, nor keep a good table with nothing to keep it on, so she wished to sell the house and retire into obscurity on the proceeds. Her brother-in-law, however, suggested paying guests; so would she be able to continue in her home, even if on a slightly different basis. Many people at that period were beginning to take in paying guests. She would not, he thought, lose caste. Especially if she restricted herself to real gentlefolk, who wouldn't allow her to feel her position.

It was a little difficult at first, but she got used to it and was doing very well when the war broke out. Then, of course, she had to stand by Dolly. So she gave up her house and guests, and her means were now very small; for somehow, remarked Mrs. Barnes, directly one wants to sell nobody seems to want to buy, and she had had to let her beautiful house go for very little—

'But why—' I interrupted; and pulled myself up.

I was just going to ask why Dolly hadn't gone to Mrs. Barnes and helped with the paying guests, instead of Mrs. Barnes giving them up and going to Dolly; but I stopped because I thought perhaps such a question, seeing that they quite remarkably refrain from asking me questions, might have been a little indiscreet at our present stage of intimacy. No, I can't call it intimacy,—friendship, then. No, I can't call it friendship either, yet; the only word at present is acquaintanceship.

August 21st.

The conduct of my guests is so extraordinarily discreet, their careful avoidance of curiosity, of questions, is so remarkable, that I can but try to imitate. They haven't asked me a single thing. I positively thrust the Dean on them. They make no comment on anything either, except the situation and the view. We seem to talk if not only certainly chiefly about that. We haven't even got to books yet. I still don't know about *The Rosary.* Once or twice when I have been alone with Mrs. Barnes she has begun to talk of Dolly, who appears to fill most of her thoughts, but each time she has broken off in the middle and resumed her praises of the situation and the view. I haven't been alone at all yet with Dolly; nor, though Mr. Barnes has dwelt upon in detail, have I been told anything about Mr. Jewks.

August 22nd.

Impetuosity sometimes gets the better of me, and out begins to rush a question; but up to now I have succeeded in catching it and strangling it before it is complete. For perhaps my new friends have been very unhappy, just as I have been very unhappy, and they may be struggling out of it just as I am, still with places in their memories that hurt too much for them to dare to touch. Perhaps it is only by silence and reserve that they can manage to be brave.

There are no signs, though, of anything of the sort on their composed faces; but then neither, I think, would they see any signs of such things on mine. The moment as it passes is, I find, somehow a gay thing. Somebody says something amusing, and I laugh; somebody is kind, and I am happy. Just the smell of a flower, the turn of a sentence, anything, the littlest thing, is enough to make the passing moment gay to me. I am sure my guests can't tell by looking at me that I have ever been anything but cheerful; and so I, by looking at them, wouldn't be able to say that they have ever been anything but composed,—Mrs. Barnes composed and grave, Mrs. Jewks composed and smiling.

But I refuse now to jump at conclusions in the nimble way I used to. Even about Mrs. Barnes, who would seem to be an untouched monument of tranquillity, a cave of calm memories, I can no longer be sure. And so we sit together quietly on the terrace, and are as presentable as so many tidy, white-curtained houses in a decent street. We don't know what we've got inside us each of disorder, of discomfort, of anxieties. Perhaps there is nothing; perhaps my friends are as tidy and quiet inside as out. Anyhow up to now we have kept ourselves to ourselves, as Mrs. Barnes would say, and we make a most creditable show.

Only I don't believe in that keeping oneself to oneself attitude. Life is too brief to waste any of it being slow in making friends. I have a theory—Mrs. Barnes isn't the only one of us three who has theories—that reticence is a stuffy, hampering thing. Except about one's extremest bitter grief, which is, like one's extremest joy of love, too deeply hidden away with God to be told of, one should be without reserves. And if one makes mistakes, and if the other person turns out to have been unworthy of being treated frankly and goes away and distorts, it can't be helped,—one just takes the risk. For isn't anything better than distrust, and the slowness and selfish fear of caution? Isn't anything better than not doing one's fellow creatures the honour of taking it for granted that they are, women and all, gentlemen? Besides, how lonely....

August 23rd.

The sun goes on blazing, and we go on sitting in the shade in a row.

Mrs. Barnes does a great deal of knitting. She knits socks for soldiers all day. She got into this habit during the war, when she sent I don't know how many pairs a year to the trenches, and now she can't stop. I suppose these will go to charitable institutions, for although the war has left off there are, as Mrs. Jewks justly said, still legs in the world.

This remark I think came under the heading Dolly in Mrs. Barnes's mind, for she let her glance rest a moment on her sister in a kind of affectionate concern.

Mrs. Jewks hasn't said much yet, but each time she has said anything I have liked it. Usually she murmurs, almost as if she didn't want Mrs. Barnes to hear, yet couldn't help saying what she says. She too knits, but only, I think, because her sister likes to see her sitting beside her doing it, and never for long at a time. Her chief occupation, I have discovered, is to read aloud to Mrs. Barnes.

This wasn't done in my presence the first four days out of consideration for me, for everybody doesn't like being read to, Mrs. Barnes explained afterwards; but they went upstairs after lunch to their rooms,—to sleep, as I supposed, knowing how well they do that, and it was only gradually that I realised, from the monotonous gentle drone coming through the window to where I lay below on the grass, that it wasn't Mrs. Barnes giving long drawn-out counsel on the best way to cope with the dangers of being Dolly, but that it was Mrs. Jewks reading aloud.

After that I suggested they should do this on the terrace, where it is so much cooler than anywhere else in the afternoon; so now, reassured that it in no way disturbs me—Mrs. Barnes's politeness and sense of duty as a guest never flags for a moment—this is what happens, and it happens in the mornings also. For, says Mrs. Barnes, how much better it is to study what persons of note have said than waste the hours of life saying things oneself.

They read biographies and histories, but only those, I gather, that are not recent; and sometimes, Mrs. Barnes said, they lighten what Mrs. Jewks described in a murmur as these more solid forms of fiction by reading a really good novel.

I asked Mrs. Barnes with much interest about the novel. What were the really good ones they had read? And I hung on the answer, for here was something we could talk about that wasn't either the situation or the view and yet was discreet.

'Ah,' she said, shaking her head, 'there are very few really good novels. We don't care, of course, except for the very best, and they don't appear to be printed nowadays.'

'I expect the very best are unprintable,' murmured Mrs. Jewks, her head bent over her knitting, for it was one of the moments when she too was engaged on socks.

'There used to be very good novels,' continued Mrs. Barnes, who hadn't I think heard her, 'but of recent years they have indeed been few. I begin to fear we shall never again see a Thackeray or a Trollope. And yet I have a theory—and surely these two writers prove it—that it is possible to be both wholesome and clever.'

'I don't want to see any more Thackerays and Trollopes,' murmured Mrs. Jewks. 'I've seen them. Now I want to see something different.'

This sentence was too long for Mrs. Barnes not to notice, and she looked at me as one who should say, 'There. What did I tell you? Her name unsettles her.'

There was a silence.

'Our father,' then said Mrs. Barnes, with so great a gravity of tone that for a moment I thought she was unaccountably and at eleven o'clock in the morning going to embark on the Lord's Prayer, 'knew Thackeray. He mixed with him.'

And as I wasn't quite sure whether this was a rebuke for Dolly or information for me, I kept quiet.

As, however, Mrs. Barnes didn't continue, I began to feel that perhaps I was expected to say something. So I did.

'That,' I said, 'must have been very—'

I searched round for an enthusiastic word, but couldn't find one. It is unfortunate how I can never think of any words more enthusiastic than what I am feeling. They seem to disappear; and urged by politeness, or a desire to please, I frantically hunt for them in a perfectly empty mind. The nearest approach to one that I found this morning was Enjoyable. I don't think much of Enjoyable. It is a watery word; but it was all I found, so I said it. 'That must have been very enjoyable,' I said; and even I could hear that my voice was without excitement.

Mrs. Jewks looked at me and smiled.

'It was more than enjoyable,' said Mrs. Barnes, 'it was elevating. Dolly used to feel just as I do about it,' she added, her eye reproachfully on her sister. 'It is not Thackeray's fault that she no longer does.'

'It's only because I've finished with him,' said Mrs. Jewks apologetically. 'Now I want something *different.*'

'Dolly and I,' explained Mrs. Barnes to me, 'don't always see alike. I have a theory that one doesn't finish with the Immortals.'

'Would you put Thackeray—' I began diffidently.

Mrs. Barnes stopped me at once.

'Our father,' she said—again my hands instinctively wanted to fold—'who was an excellent judge, indeed a specialist if I may say so, placed him among the Immortals. Therefore I am content to leave him there.'

'But isn't that filial piety rather than—' I began again, still diffident but also obstinate.

'In any case,' interrupted Mrs. Barnes, raising her hand as though I were the traffic, 'I shall never forget the influence he and the other great writers of the period had upon the boys.'

'The boys?' I couldn't help inquiring, in spite of this being an interrogation.

'Our father educated boys. On an unusual and original system. Being devoid of the classics, which he said was all the better because then he hadn't to spend any time remembering them, he was a devoted English linguist. Accordingly he taught boys English,—foreign boys, because English boys naturally know it already, and his method was to make them minutely acquainted with the great novels,—the great wholesome novels of that period. Not a French, or Dutch, or Italian boy but went home—'

'Or German,' put in Mrs. Jewks. 'Most of them were Germans.'

Mrs. Barnes turned red. 'Let us forget them,' she said, with a wave of her hand. 'It is my earnest desire,' she continued, looking at me, 'to forget Germans.'

'Do let us,' I said politely.

'Not one of the boys,' she then went on, 'but returned to his country with a knowledge of the colloquial English of the best period, and of the noble views of that period

30

as expressed by the noblest men, unobtainable by any other method. Our father called himself a Non-Grammarian. The boys went home knowing no rules of grammar, yet unable to talk incorrectly. Thackeray himself was the grammar, and his characters the teachers. And so was Dickens, but not quite to the same extent, because of people like Sam Weller who might have taught the boys slang. Thackeray was immensely interested when our father wrote and told him about the school, and once when he was in London he invited him to lunch.'

Not quite clear as to who was in London and which invited which, I said, 'Who?'

'It was our father who went to London,' said Mrs. Barnes, 'and was most kindly entertained by Thackeray.'

'He went because he wasn't there already,' explained Mrs. Jewks.

'Dolly means,' said Mrs. Barnes, 'that he did not live in London. Our father was an Oxford man. Not in the narrow, technical meaning that has come to be attached to the term, but in the simple natural sense of living there. It was there that we were born, and there that we grew up in an atmosphere of education. We saw it all round us going on in the different colleges, and we saw it in detail and at first hand in our own home. For we too were brought up on Thackeray and Dickens, in whom our father said we would find everything girls needed to know and nothing that, they had better not.'

'I used to have a perfect *itch*,' murmured Mrs. Jewks, 'to know the things I had better not.'

And Mrs. Barnes again looked at me as one who should say, 'There. What did I tell you? Such a word, too. Itch.'

There was a silence. I could think of nothing to say that wouldn't appear either inquisitive or to be encouraging Dolly.

Mrs. Barnes sits between us. This arrangement of our chairs on the grass happened apparently quite naturally the first day, and now has become one that I feel I mustn't disturb. For me to drop into the middle chair would somehow now be impossible. It is Mrs. Barnes's place. Yet I do want to sit next to Mrs. Jewks and talk to her. Or better still, go for a walk with her. But Mrs. Barnes always goes for the walks, either with or without me, but never without Mrs. Jewks. She hasn't yet left us once alone together. If anything needs fetching it is Mrs. Jewks who fetches it. They don't seem to want to write letters, but if they did I expect they would both go in to write them at the same time.

I do think, though, that we are growing a little more intimate. At least to-day we have talked of something that wasn't the view. I shouldn't be surprised if in another week, supposing the hot weather lasts so long, I shall be asking Mrs. Barnes outright what it is Dolly did that has apparently so permanently unnerved her sister.

But suppose she retaliated by asking me,—oh, there are so many things she could ask me that I couldn't answer! Except with the shameful, exposing answer of beginning very helplessly to cry....

August 24th.

Last night I ran after Mrs. Jewks just as she was disappearing into her room and said, 'I'm going to call you Dolly. I don't like Jewks. How do you spell it?'

'What—Dolly?' she asked, smiling.

'No—Jewks.'

But Mrs. Barnes came out of her bedroom and said, 'Did we forget to bid you goodnight? How very remiss of us.'

And we all smiled at each other, and went into our rooms, and shut the doors.

August 25th.

The behaviour of time is a surprising thing. I can't think how it manages to make weeks sometimes seem like minutes and days sometimes seem like years. Those weeks I was here alone seemed not longer than a few minutes. These days since my guests came seem to have gone on for months.

I suppose it is because they have been so tightly packed. Nobody coming up the path and seeing the three figures sitting quietly on the terrace, the middle one knitting, the right-hand one reading aloud, the left-hand one sunk apparently in stupor, would guess that these creatures' days were packed. Many an honest slug stirred by creditable desires has looked more animate than we. Yet the days *are*packed. Mine, at any rate, are. Packed tight with an immense monotony.

Every day we do exactly the same things: breakfast, read aloud; lunch, read aloud; tea, go for a walk; supper, read aloud; exhaustion; bed. How quick and short it is to write down, and how endless to live. At meals we talk, and on the walk we talk, or rather we say things. At meals the things we say are about food, and on the walk they are about mountains. The rest of the time we don't talk, because of the reading aloud. That fills up every gap; that muzzles all conversation.

I don't know whether Mrs. Barnes is afraid I'll ask questions, or whether she is afraid Dolly will start answering questions that I haven't asked; I only know that she seems to have decided that safety lies in putting an extinguisher on talk. At the same time she is most earnest in her endeavours to be an agreeable guest, and is all politeness; but so am I, most earnest for my part in my desire to be an agreeable hostess, and we are both so dreadfully polite and so horribly considerate that things end by being exactly as I would prefer them not to be.

For instance, finding Merivale—it is Merivale's *History of the Romans under the Empire* that is being read—finding him too much like Gibbon gone sick and filled with water, a Gibbon with all the kick taken out of him, shorn of his virility and his foot-notes, yesterday I didn't go and sit on the terrace after breakfast, but took a volume of the authentic Gibbon and departed by the back door for a walk.

It is usually, I know, a bad sign when a hostess begins to use the back door, but it wasn't a sign of anything in this case except a great desire to get away from Merivale. After lunch, when, strengthened by my morning, I prepared to listen to some more of him, I found the chairs on the terrace empty, and from the window of Mrs. Barnes's room floated down the familiar muffled drone of the first four days.

So then I went for another walk, and thought. And the result was polite affectionate protests at tea-time, decorated with some amiable untruths about domestic affairs having called me away—God forgive me, but I believe I said it was the laundress—and such real distress on Mrs. Barnes's part at the thought of having driven me off my own terrace, that now so as to shield her from thinking anything so painful to her I must needs hear Merivale to the end.

'Dolly,' I said, meeting her by some strange chance alone on the stairs going down to supper—invariably the sisters go down together—'do you like reading aloud?'

I said it very quickly and under my breath, for at the bottom of the stairs would certainly be Mrs. Barnes.

'No,' she said, also under her breath.

'Then why do you do it?'

'Do you like listening?' she whispered, smiling.

'No,' I said.

'Then why do you do it?'

'Because—' I said. 'Well, because—'

She nodded and smiled. 'Yes,' she whispered, 'that's my reason too.'

August 26th.

All day to-day I have emptied myself of any wishes of my own and tried to be the perfect hostess. I have given myself up to Mrs. Barnes, and on the walk I followed where she led, and I made no suggestions when paths crossed though I have secret passionate preferences in paths, and I rested on the exact spot she chose in spite of knowing there was a much prettier one just round the corner, and I joined with her in admiring a view I didn't really like. In fact I merged myself in Mrs. Barnes, sitting by her on the mountain side in much the spirit of Wordsworth, when he sat by his cottage fire without ambition, hope or aim.

August 27th.

The weather blazes along in its hot beauty. Each morning, the first thing I see when I open my eyes is the great patch of golden light on the wall near my bed that means another perfect day. Nearly always the sky is cloudless—a deep, incredible blue. Once or twice, when I have gone quite early to my window towards the east, I have seen what looked to my sleepy eyes like a flock of little angels floating slowly along the tops of the mountains, or at any rate, if not the angels themselves, delicate bright tufts of feathers pulled out of their wings. These objects, on waking up more completely, I have perceived to be clouds; and then I have thought that perhaps that day there would be rain. But there never has been rain.

The clouds have floated slowly away to Italy, and left us to another day of intense, burning heat.

I don't believe the weather will ever break up. Not, anyhow, for a long time. Not, anyhow, before I have heard Merivale to the end.

August 28th.

In the morning when I get up and go and look out of my window at the splendid east I don't care about Merivale. I defy him. And I make up my mind that though my body may be present at the reading of him so as to avoid distressing Mrs. Barnes and driving her off the terrace—we are minute in our care not to drive each other off the terrace—my ears shall be deaf to him and my imagination shall wander. Who is Merivale, that he shall burden my memory with even shreds of his unctuous imitations? And I go down to breakfast with a fortified and shining spirit, as one who has arisen refreshed and determined from prayer, and out on the terrace I do shut my ears. But I think there must be chinks in them, for I find my mind is much hung about, after all, with Merivale. Bits like this.

Propertius is deficient in that light touch and exquisitely polished taste which volatilize the sensuality and flattery of Horace. The playfulness of the Sabine bard is that of the lapdog, while the Umbrian reminds us of the pranks of a clumsier and less tolerated quadruped.

This is what you write if you want to write like Gibbon, and yet remain at the same time a rector and chaplain to the Speaker of the House of Commons; and this bit kept on repeating itself in my head like a tune during luncheon to-day. It worried me that I couldn't decide what the clumsier and less tolerated quadruped was.

'A donkey,' said Mrs. Jewks, on my asking my guests what they thought.

'Surely yes—an ass,' said Mrs. Barnes, whose words are always picked.

'But why should a donkey be less tolerated than a lapdog?' I asked. 'I would tolerate it more. If I might tolerate only one, it would certainly be the donkey.'

'Perhaps he means a flea,' suggested Mrs. Jewks.

'Dolly,' said Mrs. Barnes.

'But fleas do go in for pranks, and are less tolerated than lapdogs,' said Mrs. Jewks.

'Dolly,' said Mrs. Barnes again.

'Except that,' I said, not heeding Mrs. Barnes for a moment in my pleasure at having got away from the usual luncheon-table talk of food, 'haven't fleas got more than four legs?'

'That's centipedes,' said Dolly.

'Then it's two legs that they've got.'

'That's birds,' said Dolly.

We looked at each other and began to laugh. It was the first time we had laughed, and once we had begun we laughed and laughed, in that foolish way one does about completely idiotic things when one knows one oughtn't to and hasn't for a long while.

There sat Mrs. Barnes, straight and rocky, with worried eyes. She never smiled; and indeed why should she? But the more she didn't smile the more we laughed,—helplessly, ridiculously. It was dreadful to laugh, dreadful to mention objects that distressed her as vulgar; and because it was dreadful and we knew it was dreadful, we couldn't stop. So was I once overcome with deplorable laughter in church, only because a cat came in. So have I seen an ill-starred woman fall a prey to unseasonable mirth at a wedding. We laughed positively to tears. We couldn't stop. I did try to. I was really greatly ashamed. For I was doing what I now feel in all my bones is the thing Mrs. Barnes dreads most,—I was encouraging Dolly.

Afterwards, when we had settled down to Merivale, and Dolly finding she had left the book upstairs went in to fetch it, I begged Mrs. Barnes to believe that I wasn't often quite so silly and didn't suppose I would be like that again.

She was very kind, and laid her hand for a moment on mine,—such a bony hand, marked all over, I thought as I looked down at it, with the traces of devotion and self-sacrifice. That hand had never had leisure to get fat. It may have had it in the spacious days of Mr. Barnes, but the years afterwards had certainly been lean ones; and since the war, since the selling of her house and the beginning of the evidently wearing occupation of what she had called standing by Dolly, the years, I understand, have been so lean that they were practically bone.

'I think,' she said, 'I have perhaps got into the way of being too serious. It is because Dolly, I consider, is not serious enough. If she were more so I would be less so, and that would be better for us both. Oh, you musn't suppose,' she added, 'that I cannot enjoy a joke as merrily as anybody.' And she smiled broadly and amazingly at me, the rockiest, most determined smile.

'There wasn't any joke, and we were just absurd,' I said penitently, in my turn laying my hand on hers. 'Forgive me. I'm always sorry and ashamed when I have behaved as though I were ten. I do try not to, but sometimes it comes upon one unexpectedly—'

'Dolly is a little old to behave as though she were ten,' said Mrs. Barnes, in sorrow rather than in anger.

'And I'm a little old too. It's very awkward when you aren't so old inside as you are outside. For years I've been trying to be dignified, and I'm always being tripped up by a kind of apparently incurable natural effervescence.'

Mrs. Barnes looked grave.

'That is what is the matter with Dolly,' she said. 'Just that. How strange that you should have met. For it isn't usual. I cannot believe it is usual. All her troubles have been caused by it. I do not, however, regard it as incurable. On the contrary—I have helped her to check it, and she is much better than she was.'

'But what are you afraid she will do *now*?' I asked; and Dolly, coming out with, the book under her arm and that funny little air of jauntiness that triumphs when she walks over her sobering black skirt and white cotton petticoat, prevented my getting an answer.

But I felt in great sympathy with Mrs. Barnes. And when, starting for our walk after tea, something happened to Dolly's boot—I think the heel came off—and she had to turn back, I gladly went on alone with her sister, hoping that perhaps she would continue to talk on these more intimate lines.

And so she did.

'Dolly,' she said almost immediately, almost before we had got round the turn of the path, 'is the object of my tenderest solicitude and love.'

'I know. I see that,' I said, sympathetically.

'She was the object of my love from the moment when she was laid, a new born baby, in the arms of the little ten year old girl I was then, and she became, as she grew up and developed the characteristics I associate with her name, the object of my solicitude. Indeed, of my concern.'

'I wish,' I said, as she stopped and I began to be afraid this once more was to be all and the shutters were going to be shut again, 'we might be real friends.'

'Are we not?' asked Mrs. Barnes, looking anxious, as though she feared she had failed somewhere in her duties as a guest.

'Oh yes—we are friends of course, but I meant by real friends people who talk together about anything and everything. *Almost* anything and everything,' I amended. 'People who tell each other things,' I went on hesitatingly. '*Most* things,' I amended.

'I have a great opinion of discretion,' said Mrs. Barnes.

'I am sure you have. But don't you think that sometimes the very essence of real friendship consists in—'

'Mr. Barnes always had his own dressing-room.'

This was unexpected, and it silenced me. After a moment I said lamely, 'I'm sure he did. But you were saying about Dol—about Mrs. Jewks—'

'Yes.' Mrs. Barnes sighed. 'Well, it cannot harm you or her,' she went on after a pause, 'for me to tell you that the first thing Dolly did as soon as she was grown up was to make an impetuous marriage.'

'Isn't that rather what most of us begin with?'

'Few are so impetuous. Mine, for instance, was not. Mine was the considered union of affection with regard, entered into properly in the eye of all men, and accompanied by the good wishes of relations and friends. Dolly's—well, Dolly's was impetuous. I cannot say ill-advised, because she asked no one's advice. She plunged—it is not too strong a word, and unfortunately can be applied to some of her subsequent movements—into a misalliance, and in order to contract it she let herself down secretly at night from her bedroom window by means of a sheet.'

Mrs. Barnes paused.

'How very—how very spirited,' I couldn't help murmuring.

Indeed I believe I felt a little jealous. Nothing in my own past approaches this in enterprise. And I not only doubted if I would ever have had the courage to commit myself to a sheet, but I felt a momentary vexation that no one had ever suggested that on his account I should. Compared to Dolly, I am a poor thing.

'So you can understand,' continued Mrs. Barnes, 'how earnestly I wish to keep my sister to lines of normal conduct. She has been much punished for her departures from them. I am very anxious that nothing should be said to her that might seem—well, that might seem to be even slightly in sympathy with actions or ways of looking at life that have in the past brought her unhappiness, and can only in the future bring her yet more.'

'But why,' I asked, still thinking of the sheet, 'didn't she go out to be married through the front door?'

'Because our father would never have allowed his front door to be used for such a marriage. You forget that it was a school, and she was running away with somebody who up till a year or two previously had been one of the pupils.'

'Oh? Did she marry a foreigner?'

Mrs. Barnes flushed a deep, painful red. She is brown and weather-beaten, yet through the brownness spread unmistakeably this deep red. Obviously she had forgotten what she told me the other day about the boys all being foreigners.

'Let us not speak evil of the dead,' she said with awful solemnity; and for the rest of the walk would talk of nothing but the view.

But in my room to-night I have been thinking. There are guests and guests, and some guests haunt one. These guests are that kind. They wouldn't haunt me so much if only we could be really friends; but we'll never be really friends as long as I am kept from talking to Dolly and between us is fixed the rugged and hitherto unscaleable barrier of Mrs. Barnes. Perhaps to-morrow, if I have the courage, I shall make a great attempt at friendship,—at what Mrs. Barnes would call being thoroughly indiscreet. For isn't it senseless for us three women, up here alone together, to spend the precious days when we might be making friends for life hiding away from each other? Why can't I be told outright that Dolly married a German? Evidently she did; and if she could bear it I am sure I can. Twenty years ago it might have happened to us all. Twenty years ago I might have done it myself, except that there wasn't the German living who would have got me to go down a sheet for him. And anyhow Dolly's German is dead; and doesn't even a German leave off being one after he is dead? Wouldn't he naturally incline, by the sheer action of time, to dissolve into neutrality? It doesn't seem humane to pursue him into the recesses of eternity as an alien enemy. Besides, I thought the war was over.

For a long while to-night I have been leaning out of my window thinking. When I look at the stars I don't mind about Germans. It seems impossible to. I believe if Mrs. Barnes would look at them she wouldn't be nearly so much worried. It is a very good practice, I think, to lean out of one's window for a space before going to bed and let the cool darkness wash over one. After being all day with people, how blessed a thing it is not to be with them. The night to-night is immensely silent, and I've been standing so quiet, so motionless that I would have heard the smallest stirring of a leaf. But nothing is stirring. The air is quite still. There isn't a sound. The mountains seem to be brooding over a valley that has gone to sleep.

August 29th.

Antoine said to me this morning that he thought if *ces dames*—so he always speaks of Mrs. Barnes and Dolly—were going to stay any time, perhaps an assistant for Mrs. Antoine had better be engaged; because Mrs. Antoine might otherwise possibly presently begin to find the combination of heat and visitors a little—

'Of course,' I said. 'Naturally she might. I regret, Antoine, that I did not think of this. Why did you not point it out sooner? I will go myself this very day and search for an assistant.'

Antoine said that such exertions were not for Madame, and that it was he who would search for the assistant.

I said he couldn't possibly leave the chickens and the cow, and that it was I who would search for the assistant.

So that is what I have been doing all day—having a most heavenly time wandering from village to village along the mountain side, my knapsack over my arm and freedom in my heart. The knapsack had food in it and a volume of Crabbe, because it was impossible to tell how long the search might last, and I couldn't not be nourished. I explained to my guests how easily I mightn't be back till the evening, I commended them to the special attentiveness of the Antoines, and off I went, accompanied by Mrs. Barnes's commiseration that I should have to be engaged on so hot a day in what she with felicitous exactness called a domestic pursuit, and trying very hard not to be too evidently pleased.

I went to the villages that lie in the direction of my lovely place of larches, and having after some search found the assistant I continued on towards the west, walking fast, almost as if people would know I had accomplished what I had come out for, and might catch me and take me home again.

As I walked it positively was quite difficult not to sing. Only hostesses know this pure joy. To feel so deep and peculiar an exhilaration you must have been having guests and still be having them. Before my guests came I might and did roam about as I chose, but it was never like to-day, never with that holiday feeling. Oh, I have had a wonderful day! Everything was delicious. I don't remember having smelt the woods so good, and there hasn't ever been anything like the deep cool softness of the grass I lay on at lunch-time. And Crabbe the delightful,—why don't people talk more about Crabbe? Why don't they read him more? I have him in eight volumes; none of your little books of selections, which somehow take away all his true flavour, but every bit of him from beginning to end. Nobody ever made so many couplets that fit in to so many occasions of one's life. I believe I could describe my daily life with Mrs. Barnes and Dolly entirely in couplets from Crabbe. It is the odd fate of his writings to have turned by the action of time from serious to droll. He decomposes, as it were, hilariously. I lay for hours this afternoon enjoying his neat couplets. He enchants me. I forget time when I am with him. It was Crabbe who made me late for supper. But he is the last person one takes out for a walk with one if one isn't happy. Crabbe is a barometer of serenity. You have to be in a cloudless mood to enjoy him. I was in that mood to-day. I had escaped.

Well, I have had my outing, I have had my little break, and have come back filled with renewed zeal to my guests. When I said good-night to-night I was so much pleased with everything, and felt so happily and comfortably affectionate, that I not only kissed Dolly but embarked adventurously on an embrace of Mrs. Barnes.

She received it with surprise but kindliness.

I think she considered I was perhaps being a little impulsive.

I think perhaps I was.

August 30th.

In the old days before the war this house was nearly always full of friends, guests, for they were invited, but they never were in or on my mind as guests, and I don't remember ever feeling that I was a hostess. The impression I now have of them is that they were all very young. But of course they weren't; some were quite as old as Mrs. Barnes, and once or twice came people even older. They all, however, had this in common, that whatever their age was when they arrived, by the time they left they were not more than twenty.

I can't explain this. It couldn't only have been the air, invigorating and inspiriting though it is, because my present guests are still exactly the same age as the first day. That is, Mrs. Barnes is. Dolly is of no age—she never was and never will be forty; but Mrs. Barnes is just as firmly fifty as she was a fortnight ago, and it only used to take those other guests a week to shed every one of their years except the first twenty.

Is it this static, rock-like quality in Mrs. Barnes that makes her remain so unchangeably a guest, that makes her unable to develope into a friend? Why must I, because she insists on remaining a guest, be kept so firmly in my proper place as hostess? I want to be friends. I feel as full of friendliness as a brimming cup. Why am I not let spill some of it? I should love to be friends with Dolly, and I would like very much to be friends with Mrs. Barnes. Not that I think she and I would ever be intimate in the way I am sure Dolly and I would be after ten minutes together alone, but we might develope a mutually indulgent affection. I would respect her prejudices, and she would forgive me that I have so few, and perhaps find it interesting to help me to increase them.

But the anxious care with which Mrs. Barnes studies to be her idea of a perfect guest forces me to a corresponding anxious care to be her idea of a perfect hostess. I find it wearing. There is no easy friendliness for us, no careless talk, no happy go-as-you-please and naturalness. And ought a guest to be so constantly grateful? Her gratitude is almost a reproach. It makes me ashamed of myself; as if I were a plutocrat, a profiteer, a bloated possessor of more than my share, a bestower of favours—of all odious things to be! Now I perceive that I never have had guests before, but only friends. For the first time I am really entertaining; or rather, owing to the something in Mrs. Barnes that induces in me a strange submissiveness, a strange acceptance of her ordering of our days, I am for the first time, not only in my own house, but in any house that I can remember where I have stayed, being entertained.

What is it about Mrs. Barnes that makes Dolly and me sit so quiet and good? I needn't ask: I know. It is because she is single-minded, unselfish, genuinely and deeply anxious for everybody's happiness and welfare, and it is impossible to hurt such goodness. Accordingly we are bound hand and foot to her wishes, exactly as if she were a tyrant.

Dolly of course must be bound by a thousand reasons for gratitude. Hasn't Mrs. Barnes given up everything for her? Hasn't she given up home, and livelihood, and country and friends to come and be with her? It is she who magnanimously bears the chief burden of Dolly's marriage. Without having had any of the joys of Siegfried—I can't think Dolly would mutter a name in her sleep that wasn't her husband's—she has spent these years of war cheerfully accepting the results of him, devoting herself to the forlorn and stranded German widow, spending her life, and what substance she has, in keeping her company in the dreary pensions of a neutral country, unable either to take her home to England or to leave her where she is by herself.

Such love and self-sacrifice is a very binding thing. If these conjectures of mine are right, Dolly is indeed bound to Mrs. Barnes, and not to do everything she wished would be impossible. Naturally she wears those petticoats, and those long, respectable black clothes: they are Mrs. Barnes's idea of how a widow should be dressed. Naturally she goes for excursions in the mountains with an umbrella: it is to Mrs. Barnes both more prudent and more seemly than a stick. In the smallest details of her life Dolly's gratitude must penetrate and be expressed. Yes; I think I understand her situation. The good do bind one very heavily in chains.

To an infinitely less degree Mrs. Barnes's goodness has put chains on me too. I have to walk very carefully and delicately among her feelings. I could never forgive myself if I were to hurt anyone kind, and if the kind person is cast in an entirely different mould from oneself, has different ideas, different tastes, a different or no sense of fun, why then God help one,—one is ruled by a rod of iron.

Just the procession each morning after breakfast to the chairs and Merivale is the measure of Dolly's and my subjection. First goes Dolly with the book, then comes Mrs. Barnes with her knitting, and then comes me, casting my eyes about for a plausible excuse for deliverance and finding none that wouldn't hurt. If I lag, Mrs. Barnes looks uneasily at me with her, 'Am I driving you off your own terrace?' look; and once when I lingered indoors on the pretext of housekeeping she came after me, anxiety on her face, and begged me to allow her to help me, for it is she and Dolly, she explained, who of course cause the extra housekeeping, and it distressed her to think that owing to my goodness in permitting them to be here I should be deprived of the leisure I would otherwise be enjoying.

'In your lovely Swiss home,' she said, her face puckered with earnestness. 'On your summer holiday. After travelling all this distance for the purpose.'

'Dear Mrs. Barnes—' I murmured, ashamed; and assured her it was only an order I had to give, and that I was coming out immediately to the reading aloud.

August 31st.

This morning I made a great effort to be simple.

Of course I will do everything in my power to make Mrs. Barnes happy,—I'll sit, walk, be read to, keep away from Dolly, arrange life for the little time she is here in the way that gives her mind most peace; but why mayn't I at the same time be natural? It is so natural to me to be natural. I feel so uncomfortable, I get such a choked sensation of not enough air, if I can't say what I want to say. Abstinence from naturalness is easily managed if it isn't to last long; every gracefulness is possible for a little while. But shut up for weeks together in the close companionship of two other people in an isolated house on a mountain one must, sooner or later, be natural or one will, sooner or later, die.

So this morning I went down to breakfast determined to be it. More than usually deep sleep had made me wake up with a feeling of more than usual enterprise. I dressed quickly, strengthening my determination by many good arguments, and then stood at the window waiting for the bell to ring.

At the first tinkle of the bell I hurry downstairs, because if I am a minute late, as I have been once or twice, I find my egg wrapped up in my table napkin, the coffee and hot milk swathed in a white woollen shawl Mrs. Barnes carries about with her, a plate over the butter in case there should be dust, a plate over the honey in case there should be flies, and Mrs. Barnes and Dolly, carefully detached from the least appearance of reproach or waiting, at the other end of the terrace being tactfully interested in the view.

This has made me be very punctual. The bell tinkles, and I appear. I don't appear before it tinkles, because of the peculiar preciousness of all the moments I can legitimately spend in my bedroom; but, if I were to, I would find Mrs. Barnes and Dolly already there.

I don't know when they go down, but they are always there; and always I am greeted with the politest solicitude from Mrs. Barnes as to how I slept. This of course draws forth a corresponding solicitude from me as to how Mrs. Barnes slept; and the first part of breakfast is spent in answers to these inquiries, and in the eulogies to which Mrs. Barnes then proceeds of the bed, and the pure air, that make the satisfactoriness of her answers possible.

From this she goes on to tell me how grateful she and Dolly are for my goodness. She tells me this every morning. It is like a kind of daily morning prayer. At first I was overcome, and, not knowing how to ward off such repeated blows of thankfulness, stumbled about awkwardly among protests and assurances. Now I receive them in silence, copying the example of the heavenly authorities; but, more visibly embarrassed than they, I sheepishly smile.

After the praises of my goodness come those of the goodness of the coffee and the butter, though this isn't any real relief to me, because their goodness is so much tangled up in mine. I am the Author of the coffee and the butter; without me they wouldn't be there at all.

Dolly, while this is going on, says nothing but just eats her breakfast. I think she might help me out a little, seeing that it happens every morning and that she must have noticed my store of deprecations is exhausted.

This morning, having made up my mind to be natural, I asked her straight out why she didn't talk.

She was in the middle of her egg, and Mrs. Barnes was in the middle of praising the great goodness of the eggs, and therefore, inextricably, of my great goodness, so that there was no real knowing where the eggs left off and I began; and taking the opportunity offered by a pause of coffee-drinking on Mrs. Barnes's part, I said to Dolly, 'Why do you not talk at breakfast?'

'Talk?' repeated Dolly, looking up at me with a smile.

'Yes. Say things. How are we ever to be friends if we don't say things? Don't you want to be friends, Dolly?'

'Of course,' said Dolly, smiling.

Mrs. Barnes put her cup down hastily. 'But are we not—' she began, as I knew she would.

'*Real* friends,' I interrupted. 'Why not,' I said, 'let us have a holiday from Merivale to-day, and just sit together and talk. Say things,' I went on, still determined to be natural, yet already a little nervous. '*Real* things.'

'But has the reading—is there any other book you would pref—do you not care about Merivale?' asked Mrs. Barnes, in deep concern.

'Oh yes,' I assured her, leaving off being natural for a moment in order to be polite, 'I like him very much indeed. I only thought—I do think—it would be pleasant for once to have a change. Pleasant just to sit and talk. Sit in the shade and—oh well, *say* things.'

'Yes,' said Dolly. 'I'd love to.'

'We might tell each other stories, like the people in the *Earthly Paradise*. But real stories. Out of our lives.'

'Yes,' said Dolly again. 'Yes. I'd love to.'

'We shall be very glad, I am sure,' said Mrs. Barnes politely, 'to listen to any stories you may like to tell us.'

'Ah, but you must tell some too—we must play fair.'

'I'd love to,' said Dolly again, her dimple flickering.

'Surely we—in any case Dolly and I—are too old to play at anything,' said Mrs. Barnes with dignity.

'Not really. You'll like it once you've begun. And anyhow I can't play by myself, can I,' I said, still trying to be gay and simple. 'You wouldn't want me to be lonely, would you.'

But I was faltering. Mrs. Barnes's eye was on me. Impossible to go on being gay and simple beneath that eye.

I faltered more and more. 'Sometimes I think,' I said, almost timidly, 'that we're wasting time.'

'Oh no, do you really?' exclaimed Mrs. Barnes anxiously. 'Do you not consider Merivale—' (here if I had been a man I would have said damn Merivale and felt better)— 'very instructive? Surely to read a good history can never be wasting time? And he is not heavy. Surely you do not find him heavy? His information is always imparted picturesquely, remarkably so. And though one may be too old for games one is fortunately never too old for instruction.'

'I don't *feel* too old for games,' said Dolly.

'Feeling has nothing to do with reality,' said Mrs. Barnes sternly, turning on her.

'I only thought,' I said, 'that to-day we might talk together instead of reading. Just for once—just for a change. If you don't like the idea of telling stories out of our lives let us just talk. Tell each other what we think of things—of the big things like—well, like love and death for instance. Things,' I reassured her, 'that don't really touch us at this moment.'

'I do not care to talk about love and death,' said Mrs. Barnes frostily.

'But why?'

'They are most unsettling.'

'But why? We would only be speculating—'

She held up her hand. 'I have a horror of the word. All speculation is abhorrent to me. My brother-in-law said to me, Never speculate.'

'But didn't he mean in the business sense?'

'He meant it, I am certain, in every sense. Physically and morally.'

'Well then, don't let us speculate. Let us talk about experiences. We've all had them. I am sure it would be as instructive as Merivale, and we might perhaps—perhaps we might even laugh a little. Don't you think it would be pleasant to—to laugh a little?'

'I'd love to,' said Dolly, her eyes shining.

'Suppose, instead of being women, we were three men—'

Mrs. Barnes, who had been stiffening for some minutes, drew herself up at this.

'I am afraid I cannot possibly suppose that,' she said.

'Well, but suppose we *were*—'

'I do not wish to suppose it,' said Mrs. Barnes.

'Well, then, suppose it wasn't us at all, but three men here, spending their summer holidays together can't you imagine how they would talk?'

'I can only imagine it if they were nice men,' said Mrs. Barnes, 'and even so but dimly.'

'Yes. Of course. Well, let us talk together this morning as if we were nice men,—about anything and everything. I can't *think*,' I finished plaintively, 'why we shouldn't talk about anything and everything.'

Dolly looked at me with dancing eyes.

Mrs. Barnes sat very straight. She was engaged in twisting the honey-spoon round and round so as to catch its last trickling neatly. Her eyes were fixed on this, and if there was a rebuke in them it was hidden from me.

'You must forgive me,' she said, carefully winding up the last thread of honey, 'but as I am not a nice man I fear I cannot join in. Nor, of course, can Dolly, for the same reason. But I need not say,' she added earnestly, 'that there is not the slightest reason why you, on your own terrace, shouldn't, if you wish, imagine yourself to be a nice—'

'Oh no,' I broke in, giving up. 'Oh no, no. I think perhaps you are right. I do think perhaps it is best to go on with Merivale.'

We finished breakfast with the usual courtesies.

I didn't try to be natural any more.

September 1st.

Dolly forgot herself this morning.

On the first of the month I pay the bills. Antoine reminded me last month that this used to be my practice before the war, and I remember how languidly I roused myself from my meditations on the grass to go indoors and add up figures. But to-day I liked it. I went in cheerfully.

'This is my day for doing the accounts,' I said to Mrs. Barnes, as she was about to form the procession to the chairs. 'They take me most of the morning, so I expect we won't see each other again till luncheon.'

'Dear me,' said Mrs. Barnes sympathetically, 'how very tiresome for you. Those terrible settling up days. How well I know them, and how I used to dread them.'

'Yes,' said Dolly—

Reines   Glück   geniesst   doch   nie
Wer zahlen soll und weiss nicht wie.

Poor Kitty. We know all about that, don't we.' And she put her arm round her sister.

Dolly had forgotten herself.

I thought it best not to linger, but to go in quickly to my bills.

Her accent was perfect. I know enough German to know that.

September 2nd.

We've been a little strained all day in our relations because of yesterday. Dolly drooped at lunch, and for the first time didn't smile. Mrs. Barnes, I think, had been rebuking her with more than ordinary thoroughness. Evidently Mrs. Barnes is desperately anxious I shouldn't know about Siegfried. I wonder if there is any way of delicately introducing Germans into the conversation, and conveying to her that I have guessed about Dolly's husband and don't mind him a bit. Why should I mind somebody else's husband? A really nice woman only minds her own. But I know of no two subjects more difficult to talk about tactfully than Germans and husbands; and when both are united, as in this case, my courage rather fails.

We went for a dreary walk this afternoon. Mrs. Barnes was watchful, and Dolly was meek. I tried to be sprightly, but one can't be sprightly by oneself.

September 3rd.

In the night there was a thunderstorm, and for the first time since I got here I woke up to rain and mist. The mist was pouring in in waves through the open windows, and the room was quite cold. When I looked at the thermometer hanging outside, I saw it had dropped twenty degrees.

We have become so much used to fine weather arrangements that the sudden change caused an upheaval. I heard much hurrying about downstairs, and when I went down to breakfast found it was laid in the hall. It was like breakfasting in a tomb, after the radiance of

40

our meals out of doors. The front door was shut; the rain pattered on the windows; and right up against the panes, between us and the world like a great grey flannel curtain, hung the mist. It might have been some particularly odious December morning in England.

'*C'est l'automne*,' said Antoine, bringing in three cane chairs and putting them round the tea-table on which the breakfast was laid.

'*C'est un avertissement*,' said Mrs. Antoine, bringing in the coffee.

Antoine then said that he had conceived it possible that Madame and *ces dames* might like a small wood fire. To cheer. To enliven.

'Pray not on our account,' instantly said Mrs. Barnes to me, very earnestly. 'Dolly and I do not feel the cold at all, I assure you. Pray do not have one on our account.'

'But wouldn't it be cosy—' I began, who am like a cat about warmth.

'I would far rather you did not have one,' said Mrs. Barnes, her features puckered.

'Think of all the wood!'

'But it would only be a few logs—'

'What is there nowadays so precious as logs? And it is far, far too early to begin fires. Why, only last week it was still August. Still the dog-days.'

'But if we're cold—'

'We should indeed be poor creatures, Dolly and I, if the moment it left off being warm we were cold. Please do not think we don't appreciate your kindness in wishing to give us a fire, but Dolly and I would feel it very much if our being here were to make you begin fires so early.'

'But—'

'Keep the logs for later on. Let me beg you.'

So we didn't have a fire; and there we sat, Mrs. Barnes with the white shawl at last put to its proper use, and all of us trying not to shiver.

After breakfast, which was taken away bodily, table and all, snatched from our midst by the Antoines, so that we were left sitting facing each other round empty space with a curious sensation of sudden nakedness, I supposed that Merivale would be produced, so I got up and pushed a comfortable chair conveniently for Dolly, and turned on the light.

To my surprise I found Mrs. Barnes actually preferred to relinquish the reading aloud rather than use my electric light in the daytime. It would be an unpardonable extravagance, she said. Dolly could work at her knitting. Neither of them needed their eyes for knitting.

I was greatly touched. From the first she has shown a touching, and at the same time embarrassing, concern not to cause me avoidable expense, but never yet such concern as this. I know what store she sets by the reading. Why, if we just sat there in the gloom we might begin to say things. I really was very much touched.

But indeed Mrs. Barnes is touching. It is because she is so touching in her desire not to give trouble, to make us happy, that one so continually does exactly what she wishes. I would do almost anything sooner than hurt Mrs. Barnes. Also I would do almost anything to calm her. And as for her adhesiveness to an unselfish determination, it is such that it is mere useless fatigue to try to separate her from it.

I have learned this gradually.

At first, most of my time at meals was spent in reassuring her that things hadn't been got specially on her and Dolly's account, and as the only other account they could have been got on was mine, my assurances had the effect of making me seem very greedy. I thought I lived frugally up here, but Mrs. Barnes must have lived so much more frugally that almost everything is suspected by her to be a luxury provided by my hospitality.

She was, for instance, so deeply persuaded that the apricots were got, as she says, specially, that at last to calm her I had to tell Mrs. Antoine to buy no more. And we all liked apricots. And there was a perfect riot of them down in the valley. After that we had red currants because they, Mrs. Barnes knew, came out of the garden; but we didn't eat them because we didn't like them.

Then there was a jug of lemonade sent in every day for lunch that worried her. During this period her talk was entirely of lemons and sugar, of all the lemons and sugar that wouldn't be being used if she and Dolly were again, in order to calm her, and rather than that she should be made unhappy, I told Mrs. Antoine to send in only water.

Cakes disappeared from tea a week ago. Eggs have survived at breakfast, and so has honey, because Mrs. Barnes can hear the chickens and has seen the bees and knows they are not things got specially. She will eat potatoes and cabbages and anything else that the garden produces with serenity, but grows restive over meat; and a leg of mutton made her miserable yesterday, for nothing would make her believe that if I had been here alone it wouldn't have been a cutlet.

'Let there be no more legs of mutton,' I said to Mrs. Antoine afterwards. 'Let there instead be three cutlets.'

I'm afraid Mrs. Antoine is scandalised at the inhospitable rigours she supposes me to be applying to my guests. My order to Antoine this morning not to light the fire will have increased her growing suspicion that I am developing into a cheese-paring Madame. She must have expressed her fears to Antoine; for the other day, when I told her to leave the sugar and lemons out of the lemonade and send in only the water, she looked at him, and as I went away I heard her saying to him in a low voice—he no doubt having told her I usedn't to be like this, and she being unable to think of any other explanation—'C'est la guerre.'

About eleven, having done little good by my presence in the hall whose cheerlessness wrung from me a thoughtless exclamation that I wished I smoked a pipe, upon which Dolly instantly said, 'Wouldn't it be a comfort,' and Mrs. Barnes said, 'Dolly,' I went away to the kitchen, pretending I wanted to ask what there was for dinner but really so as to be for a few moments where there was a fire.

Mrs. Antoine watched me warming myself with respectful disapproval.

'Madame devrait faire faire un peu de feu dans la halle,' she said. 'Ces dames auront bien froid.'

'Ces dames won't let me,' I tried to explain in the most passionate French I could think of. 'Ces dames implore me not to have a fire. Ces dames reject a fire. Ces dames defend themselves against a fire. I perish because of the resolve of ces dames not to have a fire.'

But Mrs. Antoine plainly didn't believe me. She thought, I could see, that I was practising a repulsive parsimony on defenceless guests. It was the sorrows of the war, she concluded, that had changed Madame's nature. This was the kindest, the only possible, explanation.

Evening.

There was a knock at my door just then. I thought it must be Mrs. Antoine come to ask me some domestic question, and said *Entrez,* and it was Mrs. Barnes.

She has not before this penetrated into my bedroom. I hope I didn't look too much surprised. I think there could hardly have been a gap of more than a second between my surprise and my recovered hospitality.

'Oh—*do* come in,' I said. 'How nice of you.'

Thus do the civilised clothe their real sensations in splendid robes of courtesy.

'Dolly and I haven't driven you away from the hall, I hope?' began Mrs. Barnes in a worried voice.

'I only came up here for a minute,' I explained, 'and was coming down again directly.'

'Oh, that relieves me. I was afraid perhaps—'

'I wish you wouldn't so often be afraid you're driving me away,' I said pleasantly. 'Do I look driven?'

But Mrs. Barnes took no notice of my pleasantness. She had something on her mind. She looked like somebody who is reluctant and yet impelled.

'I think,' she said solemnly, 'that if you have a moment to spare it might be a good opportunity for a little talk. I would like to talk with you a little.'

And she stood regarding me, her eyes full of reluctant but unconquerable conscientiousness.

'Do,' I said, with polite enthusiasm. 'Do.'

This was the backwash, I thought, of Dolly's German outbreak the other day, and Siegfried was going at last to be explained to me.

'Won't you sit down in this chair?' I said, pushing a comfortable one forward, and then sitting down myself on the edge of the sofa.

'Thank you. What I wish to say is—'

42

She hesitated. I supposed her to be finding it difficult to proceed with Siegfried, and started off impulsively to her rescue.

'You know, I don't mind a bit about—' I began.

'What I wish to say is,' she went on again, before I had got out the fatal word, 'what I wish to point out to you—is that the weather has considerably cooled.'

This was so remote from Siegfried that I looked at her a moment in silence. Then I guessed what was coming, and tried to put it off.

'Ah,' I said—for I dreaded, the grateful things she would be sure to say about having been here so long—'you do want a fire in the hall after all, then.'

'No, no. We are quite warm enough, I assure you. A fire would distress us. What I wish to say is—' Again she hesitated, then went on more firmly, 'Well, I wish to say that the weather having broken and the great heat having come to an end, the reasons which made you extend your kind, your delightful hospitality to us, have come to an end also. I need hardly tell you that we never, never shall be able to express to you—'

'Oh, but you're not going to give me notice?' I interrupted, trying to be sprightly and to clamber over her rock-like persistence in gratitude with the gaiety of a bright autumnal creeper. This was because I was nervous. I grow terribly sprightly when I am nervous.

But indeed I shrink from Mrs. Barnes's gratitude. It abases me to the dust. It leaves me mourning in much the same way that Simon Lee's gratitude left Wordsworth mourning. I can't bear it. What a world it is, I want to cry out,—what a miserable, shameful, battering, crushing world, when so dreadfully little makes people so dreadfully glad!

Then it suddenly struck me that the expression giving notice might not be taken by Mrs. Barnes, she being solemn, in the spirit in which it was offered by me, I being sprightly; and, desperately afraid of having possibly offended her, I seized on the first thing I could think of as most likely to soothe her, which was an extension, glowing and almost indefinite, of my invitation. 'Because, you know,' I said, swept along by this wish to prevent a wound, 'I won't accept the notice. I'm not going to let you go. That is, of course,' I added, 'if you and Dolly don't mind the quiet up here and the monotony. Won't you stay on here till I go away myself?'

Mrs. Barnes opened her mouth to speak, but I got up quickly and crossed over to her and kissed her. Instinct made me go and kiss her, so as to gain a little time, so as to put off the moment of having to hear whatever it was she was going to say; for whether she accepted the invitation or refused it, I knew there would be an equally immense, unbearable number of grateful speeches.

But when I went over and kissed her Mrs. Barnes put her arm round my neck and held me tight; and there was something in this sudden movement on the part of one so chary of outward signs of affection that made my heart give a little leap of response, and I found myself murmuring into her ear—amazing that I should be murmuring into Mrs. Barnes's ear—'Please don't go away and leave me—please don't—please stay—'

And as she didn't say anything I kissed her again, and again murmured, 'Please—'

And as she still didn't say anything I murmured, 'Won't you? Say you will—'

And then I discovered to my horror that why she didn't say anything was because she was crying.

I have been slow and unimaginative about Mrs. Barnes. Having guessed that Dolly was a German widow I might so easily have guessed the rest: the poverty arising out of such a situation, the vexations and humiliations of the attitude of people in the pensions she has dragged about in during and since the war,—places in which Dolly's name must needs be registered and her nationality known; the fatigue and loneliness of such a life, with no home anywhere at all, forced to wander and wander, her little set at Dulwich probably repudiating her because of Dolly; or scolding her, in rare letters, for the folly of her sacrifice; with nothing to go back, to and nothing to look forward to, and the memory stabbing her always of the lost glories of that ordered life at home in her well-found house, with the church bells ringing on Sundays, and everybody polite, and a respectful crossing-sweeper at the end of the road.

All her life Mrs. Barnes has been luminously respectable. Her respectability has been, I gather from things she has said, her one great treasure. To stand clear and plain before her friends, without a corner in her actions that needed defending or even explaining, was what the word happiness meant to her. And now here she is, wandering about in a kind of hiding. With Dolly. With the beloved, the difficult, the unexplainable Dolly. Unwelcomed, unwanted, and I daresay quite often asked by the many pension proprietors who are angrily anti-German to go somewhere else.

I have been thick-skinned about Mrs. Barnes. I am ashamed. And whether I have guessed right or wrong she shall keep her secrets. I shall not try again, however good my silly intentions may seem to me, however much I may think it would ease our daily intercourse, to blunder in among things about which she wishes to be silent. When she cried like that this morning, after a moment of looking at her bewildered and aghast, I suddenly understood. I knew what I have just been writing as if she had told me. And I stroked her hand, and tried to pretend I didn't notice anything, because it was so dreadful to see how she, for her part, was trying so very hard to pretend she wasn't crying. And I kept on saying—for indeed I didn't know what to say—'Then you'll stay—how glad I am—then that's settled—'

And actually I heard myself expressing pleasure at the certainty of my now hearing Merivale to a finish!

How the interview ended was by my conceiving the brilliant idea of going away on the pretext of giving an order, and leaving Mrs. Barnes alone in my room till she should have recovered sufficiently to appear downstairs.

'I must go and tell Mrs. Antoine something,' I suddenly said,—'something I've forgotten.' And I hurried away.

For once I had been tactful. Wonderful. I couldn't help feeling pleased at having been able to think of this solution to the situation. Mrs. Barnes wouldn't want Dolly to see she had been crying. She would stay up quietly in my room till her eyes had left off being red, and would then come down as calm and as ready to set a good example as ever.

Continuing to be tactful, I avoided going into the hall, because in it was Dolly all by herself, offering me my very first opportunity for the talk alone with her that I have so long been wanting; but of course I wouldn't do anything now that might make Mrs. Barnes uneasy; I hope I never may again.

To avoid the hall, however, meant finding myself in the servants' quarters. I couldn't take shelter in the kitchen and once more warm myself, because it was their dinner hour. There remained the back door, the last refuge of a hostess. It was open; and outside was the yard, the rain, and Mou-Mou's kennel looming through the mist.

I went and stood in the door, contemplating what I saw, waiting till I thought Mrs. Barnes would have had time to be able to come out of my bedroom. I knew she would stay there till her eyes were ready to face the world again, so I knew I must have patience. Therefore I stood in the door and contemplated what I saw from it, while I sought patience and ensued it. But it is astonishing how cold and penetrating these wet mountain mists are. They seem to get right through one's body into one's very spirit, and make it cold too, and doubtful of the future.

September 4th.

Dolly looked worried, I thought, yesterday when Mrs. Barnes, as rocky and apparently arid as ever—but I knew better—told her at tea-time in my presence that I had invited them to stay on as long as I did.

There were fortunately few expressions of gratitude this time decorating Mrs. Barnes's announcement. I think she still wasn't quite sure enough of herself to be anything but brief. Dolly looked quickly at me, without her usual smile. I said what a great pleasure it was to know they weren't going away. 'You do like staying, don't you, Dolly?' I asked, breaking off suddenly in my speech, for her serious eyes were not the eyes of the particularly pleased.

She said she did; of course she did; and added the proper politenesses. But she went on looking thoughtful, and I believe she wants to tell me, or have me told by Mrs. Barnes, about Siegfried. I think she thinks I ought to know what sort of guest I've got before deciding whether I really want her here any longer or not.

44

I wish I could somehow convey to Dolly, without upsetting Mrs. Barnes, that I do know and don't mind. I tried to smile reassuringly at her, but the more I smiled the more serious she grew.

As for Mrs. Barnes, there is now between her and me the shyness, the affection, of a secret understanding. She may look as arid and stiff as she likes, but we have kissed each other with real affection and I have felt her arm tighten round my neck. How much more enlightening, how much more efficacious than any words, than any explanations, is that very simple thing, a kiss. I believe if we all talked less and kissed more we should arrive far quicker at comprehension. I give this opinion with diffidence. It is rather a conjecture than an opinion. I have not found it shared in literature—in conversation I would omit it—except once, and then by a German. He wrote a poem whose first line was:

O schwöre nicht und küsse nur

And I thought it sensible advice.

September 5th.

The weather after all hasn't broken. We have had the thunderstorm and the one bad day, and then it cleared up. It didn't clear up back to heat again—this year there will be no more heat—but to a kind of cool, pure gold. All day yesterday it was clearing up, and towards evening there came a great wind and swept the sky clear during the night of everything but stars; and when I woke this morning there was the familiar golden patch on the wall again, and I knew the day was to be beautiful.

And so it has been, with the snow come much lower down the mountains, and the still air very fresh. Things sparkle; and one feels like some bright bubble of light oneself. Actually even Mrs. Barnes has almost been like that,—has been, for her, astonishingly, awe-inspiringly gay.

'Ah,' she said, standing on the terrace after breakfast, drawing in deep draughts of air, 'now I understand the expression so frequently used in descriptions of scenery. This air indeed is like champagne.'

'It does make one feel very healthy,' I said.

There were several things I wanted to say instead of this, things suggested by her remark, but I refrained. I mean to be careful now to let my communications with Mrs. Barnes be Yea, yea and Nay, nay—that is, straightforward and brief, with nothing whatever in them that might directly or indirectly lead to the encouragement of Dolly. Dolly has been trying to catch me alone. She has tried twice since Mrs. Barnes yesterday at tea told her I had asked them to stay on, but I have avoided her.

'Healthy?' repeated Mrs. Barnes. 'It makes one feel more than healthy. It goes to one's head. I can imagine it turning me quite dizzy—quite turning my head.'

And then she actually asked me a riddle—Mrs. Barnes asked a riddle, at ten o'clock in the morning, asked me, a person long since callous to riddles and at no time since six years old particularly appreciative of them.

Of course I answered wrong. Disconcerted, I impetuously hazarded Brandy as the answer, when it should have been Whisky; but really I think it was wonderful to have got even so near the right answer as Brandy. I won't record the riddle. It was old in Mrs. Barnes's youth, for she told me she had it from her father, who, she said, could enjoy a joke as heartily as she can herself.

But what was so surprising was that the effect of the crisp, sunlit air on Mrs. Barnes should be to engender riddles. It didn't do this to my pre-war guests. They grew young, but not younger than twenty. Mrs. Barnes to-day descended to the age of bibs. I never could have believed it of her. I never could have believed she would come so near what I can only call an awful friskiness. And it wasn't just this morning, in the first intoxication of the splendid new air; it has gone on like it all day. On the mountain slopes, slippery now and difficult to walk on because of the heavy rain of the thunderstorm, might have been seen this afternoon three figures, two black ones and a white one, proceeding for a space in a rather wobbly single file, then pausing in an animated group, then once more proceeding. When they paused it was because Mrs. Barnes had thought of another riddle. Dolly was very quick at the answers,—so quick that I suspected her of having been brought up on these very ones, as she no doubt was, but I cut a lamentable figure. I tried to make up for my natural incapacity by great goodwill. Mrs. Barnes's spirits were too rare and precious, I felt, not to be welcomed; and having failed in answers I desperately ransacked my memory in search of questions, so that I could ask riddles too.

But by a strange perversion of recollection I could remember several answers and not their questions. In my brain, on inquiry, were fixed quite firmly things like this,—obviously answers to what once had been riddles.

Because	his	tail	comes	out	of	his	head.
So		did	the		other		donkey.
He	took	a	fly	and		went	home.
Orleans.							

Having nothing else to offer Mrs. Barnes I offered her these, and suggested she should supply the questions.

She thought this way of dealing with riddles subversive and difficult. Dolly began to laugh. Mrs. Barnes, filled with the invigorating air, actually laughed too. It was the first time I have heard her laugh. I listened with awe. Evidently she laughs very rarely, for Dolly looked so extraordinarily pleased; evidently her doing it made to-day memorable, for Dolly's face, turned to her sister in a delighted surprise, had the expression on it that a mother's has when her offspring suddenly behaves in a way unhoped for and gratifying.

So there we stood, gesticulating gaily on the slippery slope.

This is a strange place. Its effects are incalculable. I suppose it is because it is five thousand feet up, and has so great a proportion of sunshine.

September 6th.

There were letters this morning from England that wiped out all the gaiety of yesterday; letters that *reminded* me. It was as if the cold mist had come back again, and blotted out the light after I had hoped it had gone for good. It was as if a weight had dropped down again on my heart, suffocating it, making it difficult to breathe, after I had hoped it was lifted off for ever. I feel sick. Sick with the return of the familiar pain, sick with fear that I am going to fall back hopelessly into it. I wonder if I am. Oh, I had such *hope* that I was better! Shall I ever get quite well again? Won't it at best, after every effort, every perseverance in struggle, be just a more or less skilful mending, a more or less successful putting together of broken bits? I thought I had been growing whole. I thought I wouldn't any longer wince. And now these letters....

Ridiculous, hateful and ridiculous, to be so little master of one's own body that one has to look on helplessly at one's hands shaking.

I want to forget. I don't want to be reminded. It is my one chance of safety, my one hope of escape. To forget—forget till I have got my soul safe back again, really my own again, no longer a half destroyed thing. I call it my soul. I don't know what it is. I am very miserable.

It is details that I find so difficult to bear. As long as in my mind everything is one great, unhappy blur, there is a chance of quietness, of gradual creeping back to peace. But details remind me too acutely, flash back old anguish too sharply focussed. I oughtn't to have opened the letters till I was by myself. But it pleased me so much to get them. I love getting letters. They were in the handwriting of friends. How could I guess, when I saw them on the breakfast-table, that they would innocently be so full of hurt? And when I had read them, and I picked up my cup and tried to look as if nothing had happened and I were drinking coffee like anybody else, my silly hand shook so much that Dolly noticed it.

Our eyes met.

I couldn't get that wretched cup back on to its saucer again without spilling the coffee. If that is how I still behave, what has been the good of being here? What has the time been but wasted? What has the cure been but a failure?

I have come up to my room. I can't stay downstairs. It would be unbearable this morning to sit and be read to. But I must try to think of an excuse, quickly. Mrs. Barnes may be up any minute to ask—oh, I am hunted!

It is a comfort to write this. To write does make one in some strange way less lonely. Yet—having to go and look at oneself in the glass for companionship,—isn't that to have reached the very bottom level of loneliness?

Evening.

The direct result of those letters has been to bring Dolly and me at last together.

She came down to the kitchen-garden after me, where I went this morning when I had succeeded in straightening myself out a little. On the way I told Mrs. Barnes, with as tranquil a face as I could manage, that I had arrangements to discuss with Antoine, and so, I was afraid, would for once miss the reading.

Antoine I knew was working in the kitchen-garden, a plot of ground hidden from the house at the foot of a steep descent, and I went to him and asked to be allowed to help. I said I would do anything,—dig, weed, collect slugs, anything at all, but he must let me work. Work with my hands out of doors was the only thing I felt I could bear to-day. It wasn't the first time, I reflected, that peace has been found among cabbages.

Antoine demurred, of course, but did at last consent to let me pick red currants. That was an easy task, and useful as well, for it would save Lisette the assistant's time, who would otherwise presently have to pick them. So I chose the bushes nearest to where he was digging, because I wanted to be near some one who neither talked nor noticed, some one alive, some one kind and good who wouldn't look at me, and I began to pick these strange belated fruits, finished and forgotten two months ago in the valley.

Then I saw Dolly coming down the steps cut in the turf. She was holding up her long black skirt. She had nothing on her head, and the sun shone in her eyes and made her screw them up as she stood still for a moment on the bottom step searching for me. I saw all this, though I was stooping over the bushes.

Then she came and stood beside me.

'You oughtn't to be here,' I said, going on picking and not looking at her.

'I know,' said Dolly.

'Then hadn't you better go back?'

'Yes. But I'm not going to.'

I picked in silence.

'You've been crying,' was what she said next.

'No,' I said.

'Perhaps not with your eyes, but you have with your heart.'

At this I felt very much like Mrs. Barnes; very much like what Mrs. Barnes must have felt when I tried to get her to be frank.

'Do you know what your sister said to me the other day?' I asked, busily picking. 'She said she has a great opinion of discretion.'

'Yes,' said Dolly. 'But I haven't.'

'And I haven't either,' I was forced to admit.

'Well then,' said Dolly.

I straightened myself, and we looked at each other. Her eyes have a kind of sweet radiance. Siegfried must have been pleased when he saw her coming down the sheet into his arms.

'You mustn't tell me anything you don't quite want to,' said Dolly, her sweet eyes smiling, 'but I couldn't see you looking so unhappy and not come and—well, stroke you.'

'There isn't anything to tell,' I said, comforted by the mere idea of being stroked.

'Yes there is.'

'Not really. It's only that once—oh well, what's the good? I don't want to think of it—I want to forget.'

Dolly nodded. 'Yes,' she said. 'Yes.'

'You see I came here to get cured by forgetting, and I thought I was cured. And this morning I found I wasn't, and it has—and it has disappointed me.'

'You musn't cry, you know,' said Dolly gently. 'Not in the middle of picking red currants. There's the man—'

She glanced at Antoine, digging.

I snuffled away my tears without the betrayal of a pocket handkerchief, and managed to smile at her.

'What idiots we go on being,' I said ruefully.

'Oh—idiots!'

Dolly made a gesture as of including the whole world.

'Does one ever grow up?' I asked.

'I don't know. I haven't.'

'But do you think one ever learns to bear pain without wanting to run crying bitterly to one's mother?'

'I think it's difficult. It seems to take more time,' she added smiling, 'than I've yet had, and I'm forty. You know I'm forty?'

'Yes. That is, I've been told so, but it hasn't been proved.'

'Oh, I never could *prove* anything,' said Dolly.

Then she put on an air of determination that would have alarmed Mrs. Barnes, and said, 'There are several other things that I am that you don't know, and as I'm here alone with you at last I may as well tell you what they are. In fact I'm not going away from these currant bushes till I *have* told you.'

'Then,' I said, 'hadn't you better help me with the currants while you tell?' And I lifted the basket across and put it on the ground between us.

Already I felt better. Comforted, cheered by Dolly's mere presence and the sweet understanding that seems to shine out from her.

She turned up her sleeves and plunged her arms into the currant bushes. Luckily currants don't have thorns, for if it had been a gooseberry bush she would have plunged her bare arms in just the same.

'You have asked us to stay on,' she began, 'and it isn't fair that you shouldn't know exactly what you are in for.'

'If you're going to tell, me how your name is spelt,' I said, 'I've guessed that already. It is Juchs.'

'Oh, you're clever!' exclaimed Dolly unexpectedly.

'Well, if that's clever,' I said modestly, 'I don't know what you would say to *some* of the things I think of.'

Dolly laughed. Then she looked serious again, and tugged at the currants in a way that wasn't very good for the bush.

'Yes. His name was Juchs,' she said. 'Kitty always did pronounce it Jewks. It wasn't the war. It wasn't camouflage. She thought it was the way. So did the other relations in England. That is when they pronounced it at all, which I should think wasn't ever.'

'You mean they called him Siegfried,' I said.

Dolly stopped short in her picking to look at me in surprise. 'Siegfried?' she repeated, her arrested hands full of currants.

'That's another of the things I've guessed,' I said proudly. 'By sheer intelligently putting two and two together.'

'He wasn't Siegfried,' said Dolly.

'Not Siegfried?'

It was my turn to stop picking and look surprised.

'And in your sleep—? And so affectionately—?' I said.

'Siegfried wasn't Juchs, he was Bretterstangel,' said Dolly. 'Did I say his name that day in my sleep? Dear Siegfried.' And her eyes, even while they rested on mine became softly reminiscent.

'But Dolly—if Siegfried wasn't your husband, ought you to have—well, do you think it was wise to be dreaming of him?'

'But he was my husband.'

I stared.

'But you said your husband was Juchs,' I said.

'So he was,' said Dolly.

'He was? Then why—I'm fearfully slow, I know, but do tell me—if Juchs was your husband why wasn't he called Siegfried?'

'Because Siegfried's name was Bretterstangel. I *began* with Siegfried.'

There was a silence. We stood looking at each other, our hands full of currants.

Then I said, 'Oh.' And after a moment I said, 'I see.' And after another moment I said, 'You *began* with Siegfried.'

I was greatly taken aback. The guesses which had been arranged so neatly in my mind were swept into confusion.

'What you've got to realise,' said Dolly, evidently with an effort, 'is that I kept on marrying Germans. I ought to have left off at Siegfried. I wish now I had. But one gets into a habit—'

'But,' I interrupted, my mouth I think rather open, 'you kept on—?'

'Yes,' said Dolly, holding herself very straight and defiantly, 'I did keep on, and that's what I want you to be quite clear about before we settle down to stay here indefinitely. Kitty can't stay if I won't. I do put my foot down sometimes, and I would about this. Poor darling—she feels desperately what I've done, and I try to help her to keep it quiet with ordinary people as much as I can—oh, I'm always letting little bits out! But I can't, I won't, not tell a friend who so wonderfully invites us—'

'*You're* not going to begin being grateful?' I interrupted quickly.

'You've no idea,' Dolly answered irrelevantly, her eyes wide with wonder at her past self, 'how difficult it is not to marry Germans once you've begun.'

'But—how many?' I got out.

'Oh, only two. It wasn't their number so much. It was their quality.'

'What—Junkers?'

'Junkers? Would you mind more if they had been? Do you mind very much anyhow?'

'I don't mind anything. I don't mind your being technically German a scrap. All I think is that it was a little—well, perhaps a little excessive to marry another German when you had done it once already. But then I'm always rather on the side of frugality. I do definitely prefer the few instead of the many and the little instead of the much.'

'In husbands as well?'

'Well yes—I think so.'

Dolly sighed.

'I wish I had been like that,' she said. 'It would have saved poor Kitty so much.'

She dropped the currants she held in her hands slowly bunch by bunch into the basket.

'But I don't see,' I said, 'what difference it could make to Kitty. I mean, once you had started having German husbands at all, what did it matter one more or less? And wasn't the second one d—I mean, hadn't he left off being alive when the war began? So I don't see what difference it could make to Kitty.'

'But that's just what you've got to realise,' said Dolly, letting the last bunch of currants drop out of her hand into the basket.

She looked at me, and I became aware that she was slowly turning red. A very delicate flush was slowly spreading over her face, so delicate that for a moment I didn't see what it was that was making her look more and more guilty, more and more like a child who has got to confess—but an honourable, good child, determined that it *will* confess.

'You know,' she said, 'that I've lived in Germany for years and years.'

'Yes,' I said. 'I've guessed that.'

'And it's different from England.'

'Yes,' I said. 'So I understand.'

'The way they see things. Their laws.'

'Yes,' I said.

Dolly was finding it difficult to say what she had to say. I thought it might help her if I didn't look at her, so I once more began to pick currants. She mechanically followed my example.

'Kitty,' she said, as we both stooped busily over the same bush, 'thinks what I did too dreadful. So did all our English relations. It's because you may think so too that I've got to tell you. Then you can decide whether you really want me here or not.'

'Dear Dolly,' I murmured, 'don't please make my blood run cold—'

'Ah, but it's forbidden in the Prayer Book.'

'What is?'

'What I did.'

'*What* did you do, Dolly?' I asked, now thoroughly uneasy; had her recklessness gone so far as to lead her to tamper with the Commandments?

Dolly tore off currants and leaves in handfuls and flung them together into the basket. 'I married my uncle,' she said.

'What?' I said, really astonished.

'Karl—that was my second husband—was Siegfried's—that was my first husband's—uncle. He was Siegfried's mother's brother—my first mother-in-law's brother. My second mother-in-law was my first husband's grandmother. In Germany you can. In Germany you do. But it's forbidden in the English Prayer Book. It's put in the Table of Kindred and Affinity that you mustn't. It's number nine of the right-hand column—Husband's Mother's Brother. And Kitty well, you can guess what Kitty has felt about it. If it had been my own uncle, my own mother's brother, she couldn't have been more horrified and heartbroken. I didn't realise. I didn't think of the effect it might have on them at home. I just did it. They didn't know till I had done it I always think it saves bother to marry first and tell afterwards. I had been so many years in Germany. It seemed quite natural. I simply stayed on in the family. It was really habit.'

She threw some currants into the basket, then faced me. 'There,' she said, looking me straight in the eyes, 'I've told you, and if you think me impossible I'll go.'

'But—' I began.

Her face was definitely flushed now, and her eyes very bright.

'Oh, I'd be sorry, sorry,' she said impetuously, 'if this ended *us*!'

'Us?'

'You and me. But I couldn't stay here and not tell you, could I. Just because you may hate it so I had to tell you. You've got a dean in your family. The Prayer Book is in your blood. And if you do hate it I shall understand perfectly, and I'll go away and take Kitty and you need never see or hear of me again, so you musn't mind saying—'

'Oh do wait a minute!' I cried. 'I don't hate it. I don't mind. I'd only hate it and mind if it was I who had to marry a German uncle. I can't imagine why anybody should ever want to marry uncles anyhow, but if they do, and they're not blood-uncles, and it's the custom of the country, why not? You'll stay here, Dolly. I won't let you go. I don't care if you've married fifty German uncles. I've loved you from the moment I saw you on the top of the wall in your funny petticoat. Why, you don't suppose,' I finished, suddenly magnificently British, 'that I'm going to let any mere *German* come between you and me?'

Whereupon we kissed each other,—not once, but several times; fell, indeed, upon each other's necks. And Antoine, coming to fetch the red currants for Lisette who had been making signs to him from the steps for some time past, stood waiting quietly till we should have done.

When he thought we had done he stepped forward and said, '*Pardon, mesdames*'—and stooping down deftly extracted the basket from between us.

As he did so his eye rested an instant on the stripped and broken branches of the currant bush.

He wasn't surprised.

September 7th.

I couldn't finish about yesterday last night. When I had got as far as Antoine and the basket I looked at the little clock on my writing-table and saw to my horror that it was nearly twelve. So I fled into bed; for what would Mrs. Barnes have said if she had seen me burning the electric light and doing what she calls trying my eyes at such an hour? It doesn't matter that they are my eyes and my light: Mrs. Barnes has become, by virtue of her troubles, the secret standard of my behaviour. She is like the eye of God to me now,—in every place. And my desire to please her and make her happy has increased a hundredfold since Dolly and I have at last, in spite of her precautions, become real friends.

We decided before we left the kitchen-garden yesterday that this was the important thing: to keep Mrs. Barnes from any hurt that we can avoid. She has had so many. She will have so many more. I understand now Dolly's deep sense of all her poor Kitty has given up and endured for her sake, and I understand the shackles these sacrifices have put on Dolly. It is a terrible burden to be very much loved. If Dolly were of a less naturally serene

50

temperament she would go under beneath the weight, she would be, after five years of it, a colourless, meek thing.

We agreed that Mrs. Barnes musn't know that I know about Dolly's marriages. Dolly said roundly that it would kill her. Mrs. Barnes regards her misguided sister as having committed a crime. It is forbidden in the Prayer Book. She brushes aside the possible Prayer Books of other countries. Therefore the word German shall never I hope again escape me while she is here, nor will I talk of husbands, and perhaps it will be as well to avoid mentioning uncles. Dear me, how very watchful I shall have to be. For the first time in his life the Dean has become unmentionable.

I am writing this before breakfast. I haven't seen Dolly alone again since the kitchen-garden. I don't know how she contrived to appease Mrs. Barnes and explain her long absence, but that she did contrive it was evident from the harmonious picture I beheld when, half an hour later, I too went back to the house. They were sitting together in the sun just outside the front door knitting. Mrs. Barnes's face was quite contented. Dolly looked specially radiant. I believe she is made up entirely of love and laughter—dangerous, endearing ingredients! We just looked at each other as I came out of the house. It is the most comforting, the warmest thing, this unexpected finding of a completely understanding friend.

September 10th.

Once you have achieved complete understanding with anybody it isn't necessary, I know, to talk much. I have been told this by the wise. They have said mere knowledge that the understanding is there is enough. They have said that perfect understanding needs no expression, that the perfect intercourse is without words. That may be; but I want to talk. Not excessively, but sometimes. Speech does add grace and satisfaction to friendship. It may not be necessary, but it is very agreeable.

As far as I can see I am never, except by the rarest chance, going to get an opportunity of talking to Dolly alone. And there are so many things I want to ask her. Were her experiences all pleasant? Or is it her gay, indomitable spirit that has left her, after them, so entirely unmarked? Anyhow the last five years can't possibly have been pleasant, and yet they've not left the shadow of a stain on her serenity. I feel that she would think very sanely about anything her bright mind touched. There is something disinfecting about Dolly. I believe she would disinfect me of the last dregs of morbidness I still may have lurking inside me.

She and Mrs. Barnes are utterly poor. When the war began Dolly was in Germany, she told me that morning in the kitchen-garden, and had been a widow nearly a year. Not Siegfried's widow: Juchs's. I find her widowhoods confusing.

'Didn't you ever have a child, Dolly?' I asked.

'No,' she said.

'Then how is it you twitched the handkerchief off your sister's sleeping face that first day and said Peep bo to her so professionally?'

'I used to do that to Siegfried. We were both quite young to begin with, and played silly games.'

'I see,' I said. 'Go on.'

Juchs had left her some money; just enough to live on. Siegfried hadn't ever had any, except what he earned as a clerk in a bank, but Juchs had had some. She hadn't married Juchs for any reason, I gathered, except to please him. It did please him very much, she said, and I can quite imagine it. Siegfried too had been pleased in his day. 'I seem to have a gift for pleasing Germans,' she remarked, smiling. 'They were both very kind to me. I ended by being very fond of them both. I believe I'd be fond of anyone who was kind. There's a good deal of the dog about me.'

Directly the war began she packed up and came to Switzerland; she didn't wish, under such circumstances, to risk pleasing any more Germans. Since her marriage to Juchs all her English relations except Kitty had cast her off, so that only a neutral country was open to her, and Kitty instantly gave up everybody and everything to come and be with her. At first her little income was sent to her by her German bank, but after the first few months it sent no more, and she became entirely dependent on Kitty. All that Kitty had was what she got from selling her house. The Germans, Dolly said, would send no money out of the country. Though the war was over she could get nothing out of them unless she went back. She would never go back. It would kill Kitty; and she too, she thought, would very likely die. Her career of pleasing Germans does seem to be definitely over.

'So you see,' she said smiling, 'how wonderful it is for us to have found *you*.'

'What I can't get over,' I said, 'is having found *you*.'

But I wish, having found her, I might sometimes talk to her.

September 12th.

We live here in an atmosphere of *combats de générosité*. It is tremendous. Mrs. Barnes and I are always doing things we don't want to do because we suppose it is what is going to make the other one happy. The tyranny of unselfishness! I can hardly breathe.

September 19th.

I think it isn't good for women to be shut up too long alone together without a man. They seem to fester. Even the noblest. Taking our intentions all round they really are quite noble. We do only want to develope in ideal directions, and remove what we think are the obstacles to this development in each other's paths; and yet we fester. Not Dolly. Nothing ever smudges her equable, clear wholesomeness; but there are moments when I feel as if Mrs. Barnes and I got much mixed up together in a sort of sticky mass. Faint struggles from time to time, brief efforts at extrication, show there is still a life in me that is not flawlessly benevolent, but I repent of them as soon as made because of the pain and surprise that instantly appear in Mrs. Barnes's tired, pathetic eyes, and hastily I engulf myself once more in goodness.

That's why I haven't written lately, not for a whole week. It is glutinous, the prevailing goodness. I have stuck. I have felt as though my mind were steeped in treacle. Then to-day I remembered my old age, and the old lady waiting at the end of the years who will want to be amused, so I've begun again. I have an idea that what will really most amuse that old lady, that wrinkled philosophical old thing, will be all the times when I was being uncomfortable. She will be so very comfortable herself, so done with everything, so entirely an impartial looker-on, that the rebellions and contortions and woes of the creature who used to be herself will only make her laugh. She will be blithe in her security. Besides, she will know the sequel, she will know what came next, and will see, I daresay, how vain the expense of trouble and emotions was. So that naturally she will laugh. 'You *silly* little thing!' I can imagine her exclaiming, 'If only you had known how it all wasn't going to matter!' And she will laugh very heartily; for I am sure she will be a gay old lady.

But what we really want here now is an occasional breath of brutality,—the passage, infrequent and not too much prolonged, of a man. If he came to tea once in a way it would do. He would be a blast of fresh air. He would be like opening a window. We have minced about among solicitudes and delicacies so very long. I want to smell the rankness of a pipe, and see the cushions thrown anyhow. I want to see somebody who doesn't knit. I want to hear Mrs. Barnes being contradicted. Especially do I want to hear Mrs. Barnes being contradicted ... oh, I'm afraid I'm still not very good!

September 20th.

The grapes are ripe down in the vineyards along the edge of the valley, and this morning I proposed that we should start off early and spend the day among them doing a grape-cure.

Mrs. Barnes liked the idea very much, and sandwiches were ordered, for we were not to come back till evening; then at the last moment she thought it would be too hot in the valley, and that her head, which has been aching lately, might get worse. The sandwiches were ready on the hall table. Dolly and I were ready too, boots on and sticks in hand. To our great surprise Mrs. Barnes, contemplating the sandwiches, said that as they had been cut they mustn't be wasted, and therefore we had better go without her.

We were astonished. We were like children being given a holiday. She kissed us affectionately when we said goodbye, as though, to mark her trust in us,—in Dolly that she wouldn't tell me the dreadful truth about herself, in me that I wouldn't encourage her in undesirable points of view. How safe we were, how deserving of trust, Mrs. Barnes naturally didn't know. Nothing that either of us could say could possibly upset the other.

'If Mrs. Barnes knew the worst, knew I knew everything, wouldn't she be happier?' I asked Dolly as we went briskly down the mountain. 'Wouldn't at least part of her daily anxiety be got rid of, her daily fear lest I *should* get to know?'

'It would kill her,' said Dolly firmly.

'But surely—'

'You mustn't forget that she thinks what I did was a crime.'

'You mean the uncle.'

'Oh, she wouldn't very much mind your knowing about Siegfried. She would do her utmost to prevent it, because of her horror of Germans and of the horror she assumes you have of Germans. But once you did know she would be resigned. The other—' Dolly shook her head. 'It would kill her,' she said again.

We came to a green slope starred thick with autumn crocuses, and sat down to look at them. These delicate, lovely things have been appearing lately on the mountain, at first one by one and then in flocks,—pale cups of light, lilac on long white stalks that snap off at a touch. Like the almond trees in the suburban gardens round London that flower when the winds are cruellest, the autumn crocuses seem too frail to face the cold nights we are having now; yet it is just when conditions are growing unkind that they come out. There they are, all over the mountain fields, flowering in greater profusion the further the month moves towards winter.

This particular field of them was so beautiful that with one accord Dolly and I sat down to look. One doesn't pass such beauty by. I think we sat quite half an hour drinking in those crocuses, and their sunny plateau, and the way the tops of the pine trees on the slope below stood out against the blue emptiness of the valley. We were most content. The sun was so warm, the air of such an extraordinary fresh purity. Just to breathe was happiness. I think that in my life I have been most blest in this, that so often just to breathe has been happiness.

Dolly and I, now that we could talk as much as we wanted to, didn't after all talk much. Suddenly I felt incurious about her Germans. I didn't want them among the crocuses. The past, both hers and mine, seemed to matter very little, seemed a stuffy, indifferent thing, in that clear present. I don't suppose if we hadn't brought an empty basket with us on purpose to take back grapes to Mrs. Barnes that we would have gone on down to the vineyards at all, but rather have spent the day just where we were. The basket, however, had to be filled; it had to be brought back filled. It was to be the proof that we had done what we said we would. Kitty, said Dolly, would be fidgeted if we hadn't carried out the original plan, and might be afraid that, if we weren't eating grapes all day as arranged, we were probably using our idle mouths for saying things she wished left unsaid.

'Does poor Kitty *always* fidget?' I asked.

'Always,' said Dolly.

'About every single thing that might happen?'

'Every single thing,' said Dolly. 'She spends her life now entirely in fear—and it's all because of me.'

'But really, while she is with me she could have a holiday from fear if we told her I knew about your uncle and had accepted it with calm.'

'It would kill her,' said Dolly once more, firmly.

We lunched in the vineyards, and our desert was grapes. We ate them for a long while with enthusiasm, and went on eating them through every degree of declining pleasure till we disliked them. For fifty centimes each the owner gave us permission to eat grapes till we died if we wished to. For another franc we were allowed to fill the basket for Mrs. Barnes. Only conscientiousness made us fill it full, for we couldn't believe anybody would really want to eat such things as grapes. Then we began to crawl up the mountain again, greatly burdened both inside and out.

It took us over three hours to get home. We carried the basket in turns, half an hour at a time; but what about those other, invisible, grapes, that came with us as well? I think people who have been doing a grape-cure should sit quiet for the rest of the day, or else walk only on the level. To have to take one's cure up five thousand feet with one is hard. Again we didn't talk; this time because we couldn't. All that we could do was to pant and to perspire.

It was a brilliant afternoon, and the way led up when the vineyards left off through stunted fir trees that gave no shade, along narrow paths strewn with dry fir needles,—the slipperiest things in the world to walk on. Through these hot, shadeless trees the sun beat on our bent and burdened figures. Whenever we stopped to rest and caught sight of each other's flushed wet faces we laughed.

'Kitty needn't have been afraid we'd *say* much,' panted Dolly in one of these pauses, her eyes screwed up with laughter at my melted state.

I knew what I must be looking like by looking at her.

It was five o'clock by the time we reached the field with the crocuses, and we sank down on the grass where we had sat in the morning, speechless, dripping, overwhelmed by grapes. For a long while we said nothing. It was bliss to lie in the cool grass and not to have to carry anything. The sun, low in the sky, slanted almost level along the field, and shining right through the thin-petalled crocuses made of each a little star. I don't know anything more happy than to be where it is beautiful with some one who sees and loves it as much as you do yourself. We lay stretched out on the grass, quite silent, watching the splendour grow and grow till, having reached a supreme moment of radiance, it suddenly went out. The sun dropped behind the mountains along to the west, and out went the light; with a flick; in an instant. And the crocuses, left standing in their drab field, looked like so many blown-out candles.

Dolly sat up.

'There now,' she said. 'That's over. They look as blind and dim as a woman whose lover has left her. Have you ever,' she asked, turning her head to me still lying pillowed on Mrs. Barnes's grapes—the basket had a lid—'seen a woman whose lover has left her?'

'Of course I have. Everybody has been left by somebody.'

'I mean *just* left.'

'Yes. I've seen that too.'

'They look exactly like that,' said Dolly, nodding towards the crocuses. 'Smitten colourless. Light gone, life gone, beauty gone,—dead things in a dead world. I don't,' she concluded, shaking her head slowly, 'hold with love.'

At this I sat up too, and began to tidy my hair and put my hat on again. 'It's cold,' I said, 'now that the sun is gone. Let us go home.'

Dolly didn't move.

'Do you?' she asked.

'Do I what?'

'Hold with love.'

'Yes,' I said.

'Whatever happens?'

'Yes,' I said.

'Whatever its end is?'

'Yes,' I said. 'And I won't even say yes *and* no, as the cautious Charlotte Brontë did when she was asked if she liked London. I won't be cautious in love. I won't look at all the reasons for saying no. It's a glorious thing to have had. It's splendid to have believed all one did believe.'

'Even when there never was a shred of justification for the belief?' asked Dolly, watching me.

'Yes,' I said; and began passionately to pin my hat on, digging the pins into my head in my vehemence. 'Yes. The thing is to believe. Not go round first cautiously on tiptoe so as to be sure before believing and trusting that your precious belief and trust are going to be safe. Safe! There's no safety in love. You risk the whole of life. But the great thing *is* to risk—to believe, and to risk everything for your belief. And if there wasn't anything there, if it was you all by yourself who imagined the beautiful kind things in the other one, the wonderful, generous, beautiful kind things, what does it matter? They weren't there, but *you* for once were capable of imagining them. You *were* up among the stars for a little, you *did* touch heaven. And when you've had the tumble down again and you're scrunched all to pieces and are just a miserable heap of blood and brokenness, where's your grit that you should complain? Haven't you seen wonders up there past all telling, and had supreme joys? It's because you were up in heaven that your fall is so tremendous and hurts so. What you've got to do is not to be killed. You've got at all costs to stay alive, so that for the rest of your days you may go gratefully, giving thanks to God that once ... you see,' I finished suddenly, 'I'm a great believer in saying thank you.'

'Oh,' said Dolly, laying her hand on my knee and looking at me very kindly, 'I'm so glad!'

'Now what are you glad about, Dolly?' I asked, turning on her and giving my hat a pull straight. And I added, my chin in the air, 'Those dead women of yours in their dead world, indeed! Ashamed of themselves—that's what they ought to be.'

'You're cured,' said Dolly.

'Cured,' I echoed.

I stared at her severely. 'Oh—I see,' I said. 'You've been drawing me out.'

'Of course I have. I couldn't bear to think of you going on being unhappy—hankering—'

'Hankering?'

Dolly got up. 'Now let's go home,' she said. 'It's my turn to carry the basket. Yes, it's a horrid word. Nobody should ever hanker. I couldn't bear it if you did. I've been afraid that perhaps—'

'Hankering!'

I got up too and stood very straight.

'Give me those grapes,' said Dolly.

'Hankering!' I said again.

And the rest of the way home, along the cool path where the dusk was gathering among the bushes and the grass was damp now beneath our dusty shoes, we walked with heads held high—hankering indeed!—two women surely in perfect harmony with life and the calm evening, women of wisdom and intelligence, of a proper pride and self-respect, kind women, good women, pleasant, amiable women, contented women, pleased women; and at the last corner, the last one between us and Mrs. Barnes's eye on the terrace, Dolly stopped, put down the basket, and laying both her arms about my shoulders kissed me.

'Cured,' she said, kissing me on one side of my face. 'Safe,' she said, kissing me on the other.

And we laughed, both of us, confident and glad. And I went up to my room confident and glad, for if I felt cured and Dolly was sure I was cured, mustn't it be true?

Hankering indeed.

September 21st.

But I'm not cured. For when I was alone in my room last night and the house was quiet with sleep, a great emptiness came upon me, and those fine defiant words of mine in the afternoon seemed poor things, poor dwindled things, like kaisers in their night-gowns. For hours I lay awake with only one longing: to creep back,—back into my shattered beliefs, even if it were the littlest corner of them. Surely there must be some corner of them still, with squeezing, habitable? I'm so small. I need hardly any room. I'd curl up. I'd fit myself in. And I wouldn't look at the ruin of the great splendid spaces I once thought I lived in, but be content with a few inches. Oh, it's cold, cold, cold, left outside of faith like this....

For hours I lay awake; and being ashamed of myself did no good, because love doesn't mind about being ashamed.

Evening.

All day I've slunk about in silence, watching for a moment alone with Dolly. I want to tell her that it was only one side of me yesterday, and that there's another, and another—oh, so many others; that I meant every word I said, but there are other things, quite different, almost opposite things that I also mean; that it's true I'm cured, but only cured in places, and over the rest of me, the rest that is still sick, great salt waves of memories wash every now and then and bite and bite....

But Dolly, who seems more like an unruffled pool of clear water to-day than ever, hasn't left Mrs. Barnes's side; making up, I suppose, for being away from her all yesterday.

Towards tea-time I became aware that Mrs. Barnes was watching me with a worried face, the well-known worried, anxious face, and I guessed she was wondering if Dolly had been indiscreet on our picnic and told me things that had shocked me into silence. So I cast about in my mind for something to reassure her, and, as I thought fortunately, very soon remembered the grapes.

'I'm afraid I ate too many grapes yesterday,' I said, when next I caught her worried, questioning eye.

Her face cleared. I congratulated myself. But I didn't congratulate myself long; for Mrs. Barnes, all motherly solicitude, inquired if by any chance I had swallowed some of the stones; and desiring to reassure her to the utmost as to the reason of my thoughtfulness, I said that very likely I had; from the feel of things; from the kind of heaviness.... And she, before I could stop her, had darted into the kitchen—these lean women are terribly nimble—and before I could turn round or decide what to do next, for by this time I was suspicious, she was back again with Mrs. Antoine and all the dreadful paraphernalia of castor oil. And I had to drink it. And it seemed hard that because I had been so benevolently desirous to reassure Mrs. Barnes I should have to drink castor oil and be grateful to her as well.

'This is petty,' I thought, sombrely eyeing the bottle,—I alluded in my mind to Fate.

But as I had to drink the stuff I might as well do it gallantly. And so I did; tossing it off with an air, after raising the glass and wishing the onlookers health and happiness in what I tried to make a pleasant speech.

Mrs. Barnes, Mrs. Antoine and Dolly stood watching me spellbound. A shudder rippled over them as the last drops slid down.

Then I came up here.

September 22nd.

Let me draw your attention, O ancient woman sitting at the end of my life, to the colour of the trees and bushes in this place you once lived in, in autumns that for you are now so far away. Do you remember how it was like flames, and the very air was golden? The hazel-bushes, do you remember them? Along the path that led down from the terrace to the village? How each separate one was like a heap of light? Do you remember how you spent to-day, the 22nd of September, 1919, lying on a rug in the sun close up under one of them, content to stare at the clear yellow leaves against the amazing sky? You've forgotten, I daresay. You're only thinking of your next meal and being put to bed. But you did spend a day to-day worth remembering. You were very content. You were exactly balanced in the present, without a single oscillation towards either the past, a period you hadn't then learned to regard with the levity for which you are now so remarkable, or to the future, which you at that time, however much the attitude may amuse you now, thought of with doubt and often with fear. Mrs. Barnes let you go to-day, having an appreciation of the privileges due to the dosed, and you took a cushion and a rug—active, weren't you— and there you lay the whole blessed day, the sun warm on your body, enfolded in freshness, thinking of nothing but calm things. Rather like a baby you were; a baby on its back sucking its thumb and placidly contemplating the nursery ceiling. But the ceiling was the great sky, with, two eagles ever so far up curving in its depths, and when they sloped their wings the sun caught them and they flashed.

It seems a pity to forget these things. They make up, after all, the real preciousness of life. But I'm afraid my writing them down won't make you *feel* any joy in them again, you old thing. You'll be too brittle and rheumaticky to be able to think of lying on the grass for a whole day except with horror. I'm beginning to dislike the idea of being forced into your old body; and, on reflection, your philosophical detachment, your incapacity to do anything but laugh at the hopes and griefs and exultations and disappointments and bitter pains of your past, seems to me very like the fixed grimace of fleshless death.

September 23rd.

Mrs. Barnes can't, however hard she tries, be with us absolutely continuously. Gaps in her attendance do inevitably occur. There was one of them to-day; and I seized it to say to Dolly across the momentarily empty middle chair—we were on the terrace and the reading was going on,—'I've not seen you alone since the grape day. I wanted to tell you that I'm not cured. I had a relapse that very night. I meant all I said to you, but I meant too, all I said to myself while I was having the relapse. You'd better know the worst. I simply intolerably hankered.'

Dolly let Merivale fall on her lap, and gazed pensively at the distant mountains across the end of the valley.

'It's only the last growlings,' she said after a moment.

'Growlings?' I echoed.

'It's only the last growlings and mutterings of a thunderstorm that's going away. Whatever it was that happened to you—you've never told me, you know, but I'm quite good at somehow knowing—was very like a thunderstorm. A violent one. It was rather brief, it raged incredibly, and then it rumbled off. Though you were flattened out while it was going on, like some otherwise promising crop—'

'Oh,' I protested; but I had to laugh.

'—still when it took itself off you missed it. I wouldn't talk like this,' she said, turning her sweet eyes to me, 'I wouldn't make fun if I weren't sure you are on the road, anyhow, to being cured. Presently you'll reach the stage when you begin to realise that falling out of love is every bit as agreeable as falling in. It is, you know. It's a wonderful feeling, that gradual restoration to freedom and one's friends.'

'You don't understand after all,' I said.

Dolly said she did.

'No. Because you talk of falling out of love. What has happened to me is far worse than that. That? That's nothing. It's what everybody is doing all the time. What has happened to me is that I've lost my faith. It has been like losing God, after years of trust in Him. I believed with all my heart. And I am desolate.'

But Dolly only shook her head. 'You're not as desolate as you were,' she said. 'Nobody who loves all this as you do—' and she turned up her face to the warm sun, blinking her eyes,—'can go on being desolate long. Besides—really, you know—look at that.'

And she pointed to the shining mountains across the valley's eastern end.

Yes. That is eternal. Beauty is eternal. When I look at that, when I am in the clear mood that, looking at the mountains, really *sees* them, all the rest, the bewilderment and crying out, the clinging and the hankering, seem indeed unworthy. Imagine, with the vast landscape of the splendid world spread out before you, not moving freely in it on and on rejoicing and praising God, but sitting quite still lamenting in one spot, stuck in sediment.

'Did you say sentiment?' asked Dolly.

'Did I say anything?' I asked in surprise, turning my head to her. 'I thought I was thinking.'

'You were doing it aloud, then,' said Dolly. 'Was the word sentiment?'

'No. Sediment.'

'They're the same thing. I hate them both.'

September 24th.

What will happen to Mrs. Barnes and Dolly when I go back to England? The weather was a little fidgety to-day and yesterday, a little troubled, like a creature that stirs fretfully in its sleep, and it set me thinking. For once the change really begins at this time of the year it doesn't stop any more. It goes on through an increasing unpleasantness winds, rain, snow, blizzards—till, after Christmas, the real winter begins, without a cloud, without a stir of the air, its short days flooded with sunshine, its dawns and twilights miracles of colour.

All that fuss and noise of snow-flurries and howling winds is only the preparation for the great final calm. The last blizzard, tearing away over the mountains, is like an ugly curtain rolling up; and behold a new world. One night while you are asleep the howls and rattlings suddenly leave off, and in the morning you look out of the window and for the first time for weeks you see the mountains at the end of the valley clear against the eastern sky, clothed in all new snow from head to foot, and behind them the lovely green where the sunrise is getting ready. I know, because I was obliged to be here through the October and November and December of the year the house was built and was being furnished. They were three most horrid months; and the end of them was heaven.

But what will become of Mrs. Barnes and Dolly when the weather does finally break up?

I can't face the picture of them spending a gloomy, half-warmed winter down in some cheap pension; an endless winter of doing without things, of watching every franc. They've been living like that for five years now. Where does Dolly get her sweet serenity from? I wish I could take them to England with me. But Dolly can't go to England. She is German. She is doomed. And Mrs. Barnes is doomed too, inextricably tied up in Dolly's fate. Of course I am going to beg them to stay on here, but it seems a poor thing to offer them, to live up here in blizzards that I run away from myself. It does seem a very doubtful offer of hospitality. I ought, to make it real, to stay on with them. And I simply couldn't. I do believe I would die if I had three months shut up with Mrs. Barnes in blizzards. Let her have everything—the house, the Antoines, all, all that I possess; but only let me go.

My spirit faints at the task before me, at the thought of the persuasions and the protests that will have to be gone through. And Dolly; how can I leave Dolly? I shall be haunted in London by visions of these two up here, the wind raging round the house, the snow piled up to the bedroom windows, sometimes cut off for a whole week from the village, because only in a pause in the blizzard can the little black figures that are peasants come sprawling over the snow with their shovels to dig one out. I know because I have been through it that first winter. But it was all new to us then, and we were a care-free, cheerful group inside the house, five people who loved each other and talked about anything they wanted to, besides being backed reassuringly by a sack of lentils and several sacks of potatoes that Antoine, even then prudent and my right hand, had laid in for just this eventuality. We made great fires, and brewed strange drinks. We sat round till far into the nights telling ghost stories. We laughed a good deal, and said just what we felt like saying. But Mrs. Barnes and Dolly? Alone up here, and undug? It will haunt me.

September 25th.

She hasn't noticed the weather yet. At least, she has drawn no deductions from it. Evidently she thinks its fitfulness, its gleams of sunshine and its uneasy cloudings over, are just a passing thing and that it soon will settle down again to what it was before. After all, she no doubt says to herself, it is still September. But Antoine knows better, and so do I, and it is merely hours now before the break-up will be plain even to Mrs. Barnes. Then the *combats de générosité* will begin. I can't, I can't stop here so that Mrs. Barnes may be justified in stopping too on the ground of cheering my solitude. I drank the castor oil solely that her mind might be at rest, but I can't develope any further along lines of such awful magnanimity. I would die.

September 26th.

To-day I smoked twelve cigarettes, only that the house should smell virile. They're not as good as a pipe for that, but they're better than the eternal characterless clean smell of unselfish women.

After each cigarette Mrs. Barnes got up unobtrusively and aired the room. Then I lit another.

Also I threw the cushions on the floor before flinging myself on the sofa in the hall; and presently Mrs. Barnes came and tidied them.

Then I threw them down again.

Towards evening she asked me if I was feeling quite well. I wasn't, because of the cigarettes, but I didn't tell her that. I said I felt very well indeed. Naturally I couldn't explain to her that I had only been trying to pretend there was a man about.

'You're sure those grape-stones—?' she began anxiously.

'Oh, certain!' I cried; and hastily became meek.

September 27th.

Oaths, now. I shrink from so much as suggesting it, but there *is* something to be said for them. They're so brief. They get the mood over. They clear the air. Women explain and protest and tiptoe tactfully about among what they think are your feelings, and there's no end to it. And then, if they're good women, good, affectionate, unselfish women, they have a way of forgiving you. They keep on forgiving you. Freely. With a horrible magnanimousness.

Mrs. Barnes insisted on forgiving me yesterday for the cigarettes, for the untidiness. It isn't a happy thing, I think, to be shut up in a small lonely house being forgiven.

September 28th.

In the night the wind shook the windows and the rain pelted against them, and I knew that when I went down to breakfast the struggle with Mrs. Barnes would begin.

It did. It began directly after breakfast in the hall, where Antoine, remarking firmly '*C'est l'hiver,*' had lit a roaring fire, determined this time to stand no parsimonious nonsense, and it has gone on all day, with the necessary intervals for recuperation.

Nothing has been settled. I still don't in the least know what to do. Mrs. Barnes's attitude is obstinately unselfish. She and Dolly, she reiterates, won't dream of staying on here unless they feel that by doing so they could be of service to me by keeping me company. If I'm not here I can't be kept company with; that, she says, I must admit.

I do. Every time she says it—it has been a day of reiterations—I admit it. Therefore, if I go they go, she finishes with a kind of sombre triumph at her determination not to give trouble or be an expense; but words fail her, she adds, (this is a delusion,) to express her gratitude for my offer, etc., and never, for the rest of their lives, will she and Dolly forget the delightful etc., etc.

What am I to do? I don't know. How lightly one embarks on marriage and on guests, and in what unexpected directions do both develope! Also, what a terrible thing is unselfishness. Once it has become a habit, how tough, how difficult to uproot. A single obstinately unselfish person can wreck the happiness of a whole household. Is it possible that I shall have to stay here? And I have so many things waiting for me in England that have to be done.

There's a fire in my bedroom, and I've been sitting on the floor staring into it for the past hour, seeking a solution. Because all the while Mrs. Barnes is firmly refusing to listen for a moment to my entreaties to use the house while I'm away, her thin face is hungry with longing to accept, and the mere talking, however bravely, of taking up the old homeless wandering again fills her tired eyes with tears.

Once I got so desperate that I begged her to stay as a kindness to me, in order to keep an eye on those patently efficient and trustworthy Antoines. This indeed was the straw-clutching of the drowning, and even Mrs. Barnes, that rare smiler, smiled.

No. I don't know what to do. How the wind screams. I'll go to bed.

September 29th.

And there's nothing to be done with Dolly either.

'You told me you put your foot down sometimes,' I said, appealing to her this morning in one of Mrs. Barnes's brief absences, 'Why don't you put it down now?'

'Because I don't want to,' said Dolly.

'But *why* not?' I asked, exasperated. 'It's so reasonable what I suggest, so easy—'

'I don't want to stay here without you,' said Dolly. 'This place *is* you. You've made it. It is soaked in you. I should feel haunted here without you. Why, I should feel lost.'

'As though you would! When we hardly speak to each other as it is—'

'But I watch you,' said Dolly, smiling, 'and I know what you're thinking. You've no idea how what you're thinking comes out on your face.'

'But if it makes your unhappy sister's mind more comfortable? If she feels free from anxiety here? If she feels you are safe here?' I passionately reasoned.

'I don't want to be safe.'

'Oh Dolly—you're not going to break out again?' I asked, as anxiously every bit as poor Mrs. Barnes would have asked.

Dolly laughed. 'I'll never do anything again that makes Kitty unhappy,' she said. 'But I do like the feeling—' she made a movement with her arms as though they were wings—'oh, I *like* the feeling of having room!'

September 30th.

The weather is better again, and there has been a pause in our strivings. Mrs. Barnes and I have drifted, tired both of us, I resting in that refuge of the weak, the putting off of making up my mind, back into talking only of the situation and the view. If Mrs. Barnes were either less good or more intelligent! But the combination of non-intelligence with goodness is unassailable. You can't get through. Nothing gets through. You give in. You are flattened out. You become a slave. And your case is indeed hopeless if the non-intelligent and good, are at the same time the victims, nobly enduring, of undeserved misfortune.

Evening.

A really remarkable thing happened to-day: I've had a prayer answered. I shall never dare pray again. I prayed for a man, any man, to come and leaven us, and I've got him.

Let me set it down in order.

This afternoon on our walk, soon after we had left the house and were struggling along against gusts of wind and whirling leaves in the direction, as it happened, of the carriage road up from the valley, Dolly said, 'Who is that funny little man coming towards us?'

And I looked, and said after a moment in which my heart stood still—for what had *he* come for?—'That funny little man is my uncle.'

There he was, the authentic uncle: gaiters, apron, shovel hat. He was holding on his hat, and the rude wind, thwarted in its desire to frolic with it, frisked instead about his apron, twitching it up, bellying it out; so that his remaining hand had all it could do to smooth the apron down again decorously, and he was obliged to carry his umbrella pressed tightly against his side under his arm.

'Not your uncle the Dean?' asked Mrs. Barnes in a voice of awe, hastily arranging her toque; for a whiff of the Church, any whiff, even one so faint as a curate, is as the breath of life to her.

'Yes,' I said, amazed and helpless. 'My Uncle Rudolph.'

'Why, he might be a German,' said Dolly, 'with a name like that.'

'Oh, but don't say so to him!' I cried. 'He has a perfect *horror* of Germans—'

And it was out before I remembered, before I could stop it. Good heavens, I thought; good heavens.

I looked sideways at Mrs. Barnes. She was, I am afraid, very red. So I plunged in again, eager to reassure her. 'That is to say,' I said, 'he used to have during the war. But of course now that the war is over it would be mere silliness—nobody minds now— nobody *ought* to mind now—'

My voice, however, trailed out into silence, for I knew, and Mrs. Barnes knew, that people do mind.

By this time we were within hail of my uncle, and with that joy one instinctively assumes on such occasions I waved my stick in exultant circles at him and called out, 'How very delightful of you, Uncle Rudolph!' And I advanced to greet him, the others tactfully dropping behind, alone.

There on the mountain side, with the rude wind whisking his clothes irreverently about, we kissed; and in my uncle's kiss I instantly perceived something of the quality of Mrs. Barnes's speeches the day I smoked the twelve cigarettes,—he was forgiving me.

'I have come to escort you home to England,' he said, his face spread over with the spirit of allowing byegones to be byegones; and in that spirit he let go of his apron in order reassuringly to pat my shoulder.

Immediately the apron bellied. His hand had abruptly to leave my shoulder so as to clutch it down again. 'You are with ladies?' he said a little distractedly, holding on to this turbulent portion of his clothing.

'Yes, Uncle Rudolph,' I replied modestly. 'I hope you didn't expect to find me with gentlemen?'

'I expected to find you, dear child, as I have always found you,—ready to admit and retrace. Generously ready to admit and retrace.'

'Sweet of you,' I murmured. 'But you should have let me know you were coming. I'd have had things killed for you. Fatted things.'

'It is not I,' he said, in as gentle a voice as he could manage, the wind being what it was, 'who am the returning prodigal. Indeed I wish for your sake that I were. My shoulders could better bear the burden than those little ones of yours.'

This talk was ominous, so I said, 'I must introduce you to Mrs. Barnes and her sister Mrs. Jewks. Let me present,' I said ceremoniously, turning to them who were now

60

fortunately near enough, 'my Uncle Rudolph to you, of whom you have often heard me speak.'

'Indeed we have,' said Mrs. Barnes, with as extreme a cordiality as awe permitted.

My uncle, obviously relieved to find his niece not eccentrically alone but flanked by figures so respectable, securely, as it were, embedded in widows, was very gracious. Mrs. Barnes received his pleasant speeches with delighted reverence; and as we went back to the house, for the first thing to do with arrivals from England is to give them a bath, he and she fell naturally into each other's company along the narrow track, and Dolly and I followed behind.

We looked at each other, simultaneously perceiving the advantages of four rather than of three. Behind Mrs. Barnes's absorbed and obsequious back we looked at each other with visions in our eyes of unsupervised talks opening before us.

'They have their uses, you see,' I said in a low voice,—not that I need have lowered it in that wind.

'Deans have,' agreed Dolly, nodding.

And my desire to laugh,—discreetly, under my breath, ready to pull my face sober and be gazing at the clouds the minute our relations should turn round, was strangled by the chill conviction that my uncle's coming means painful things for me.

He is going to talk to me; talk about what I am trying so hard not to think of, what I really am succeeding in not thinking of; and he is going to approach the desolating subject in, as he will say and perhaps even persuade himself to believe, a Christian spirit, but in what really is a spirit of sheer worldliness. He has well-founded hopes of soon going to be a bishop. I am his niece. The womenkind of bishops should be inconspicuous, should see to it that comment cannot touch them. Therefore he is going to try to get me to deliver myself up to a life of impossible wretchedness again, only that the outside of it may look in order. The outside of the house,—of the house of a bishop's niece,—at all costs keep it neat, keep it looking like all the others in the street; so shall nobody know what is going on inside, and the neighbours won't talk about one's uncle.

If I were no relation but just a mere ordinary stranger-soul in difficulties, he, this very same man, would be full of understanding, would find himself unable, indeed, the facts being what they are, to be anything but most earnestly concerned to help me keep clear of all temptations to do what he calls retrace. And at the same time he would be concerned also to strengthen me in that mood which is I am sure the right one, and does very often recur, of being entirely without resentment and so glad to have the remembrance at least of the beautiful things I believed in. But I am his niece. He is about to become a bishop. Naturally he has to be careful not to be too much like Christ.

Accordingly I followed uneasily in his footsteps towards the house, dreading what was going to happen next. And nothing has happened next. Not yet, anyhow. I expect to-morrow....

We spent a most bland evening. I'm as sleepy and as much satiated by ecclesiastical good things as though I had been the whole day in church. My uncle, washed, shaven, and restored by tea, laid himself out to entertain. He was the decorous life of the party. He let himself go to that tempered exuberance with which good men of his calling like to prove that they really are not so very much different from other people after all. Round the hall fire we sat after tea, and again after supper, Dolly and I facing each other at the corners, my uncle and Mrs. Barnes in the middle, and the room gently echoed with seemly and strictly wholesome mirth. 'How enjoyable,' my uncle seemed to say, looking at us at the end of each of his good stories, gathering in the harvest of our appreciation, 'how enjoyable is the indulgence of legitimate fun. Why need one ever indulge in illegitimacy?'

And indeed his stories were so very good that every one of them, before they reached the point of bringing forth their joke, must have been to church and got married.

Dolly sat knitting, the light shining on her infantile fair hair, her eyes downcast in a dove-like meekness. Punctually her dimple flickered out at the right moment in each anecdote. She appeared to know by instinct where to smile; and several times I was only aware that the moment had come by happening to notice her dimple.

61

As for Mrs. Barnes, for the first time since I have known her, her face was cloudless. My uncle, embarked on anecdote, did not mention the war. We did not once get on to Germans. Mrs. Barnes could give herself up to real enjoyment. She beamed. She was suffused with reverential delight. And her whole body, the very way she sat in her chair, showed an absorption, an eagerness not to miss a crumb of my uncle's talk, that would have been very gratifying to him if he were not used to just this. It is strange how widows cling to clergymen. Ever since I can remember, like the afflicted Margaret's apprehensions in Wordsworth's poem, they have come to Uncle Rudolph in crowds. My aunt used to raise her eyebrows and ask me if I could at all tell her what they saw in him.

When we bade each other goodnight there was something in Mrs. Barnes's manner to me that showed me the presence of a man as already doing its work. She was aerated. Fresh, air had got into her and was circulating freely. At my bedroom door she embraced me with warm and simple heartiness, without the usual painful search of my face to see if by any chance there was anything she had left undone in her duty of being unselfish. My uncle's arrival has got her thoughts off me for a bit. I knew that what we wanted was a man. Not that a dean is quite my idea of a man, but then on the other hand neither is he quite my idea of a woman, and his arrival does put an end for the moment to Mrs. Barnes's and my dreadful *combats de générosité*. He infuses fresh blood into our anaemic little circle. Different blood, perhaps I should rather say; the blood of deans not being, I think, ever very fresh.

'Good night, Uncle Rudolph,' I said, getting up at ten o'clock and holding up my face to him. 'We have to thank you for a delightful evening.'

'Most delightful,' echoed Mrs. Barnes enthusiastically, getting up too and rolling up her knitting.

My uncle was gratified. He felt he had been at his best, and that his best had been appreciated.

'Good night, dear child,' he said, kissing my offered cheek. 'May the blessed angels watch about your bed.'

'Thank you, Uncle Rudolph,' I said, bowing my head beneath this benediction.

Mrs. Barnes looked on at the little domestic scene with reverential sympathy. Then her turn came.

'*Good* night, Mrs. Barnes,' said my uncle most graciously, shaking hands and doing what my dancing mistress used to call bending from the waist.

And to Dolly, '*Good* night, Miss—'

Then he hesitated, groping for the name. 'Mrs.,' said Dolly, sweetly correcting him, her hand in his.

'Ah, I beg your pardon. Married. These introductions—especially in that noisy wind.'

'No—not exactly married,' said Dolly, still sweetly correcting him, her hand still in his. 'Not exactly—?'

'My sister has lost her—my sister is a widow,' said Mrs. Barnes hastily and nervously; alas, these complications of Dolly's!

'Indeed. Indeed. Sad, sad,' said my uncle sympathetically, continuing to hold her hand. 'And so young. Ah. Yes. Well, good night then, Mrs—'

But again he had to pause and grope.

'Jewks,' said Dolly sweetly.

'Forgive me. You may depend I shall not again be so stupid. Good night. And may the blessed angels—'

A third time he stopped; pulled up, I suppose, by the thought that it was perhaps not quite seemly to draw the attention of even the angels to an unrelated lady's bed. So he merely very warmly shook her hand, while she smiled a really heavenly smile at him.

We left him standing with his back to the fire watching us go up the stairs, holding almost tenderly, for one must expend one's sympathy on something, a glass of hot water.

My uncle is very sympathetic. In matters that do not touch his own advancement he is all sympathy. That is why widows like him, I expect. My aunt would have known the reason if she hadn't been his wife.

October 1st.

While I dress it is my habit to read. Some book is propped up open against the looking-glass, and sometimes, for one's eyes can't be everywhere at once, my hooks in consequence don't get quite satisfactorily fastened. Indeed I would be very neat if I could, but there are other things. This morning the book was the Bible, and in it I read, *A prudent man*—how much more prudently, then, a woman—*foreseeth the evil and hideth himself, but the simple pass on and are punished.*

This made me late for breakfast. I sat looking out of the window, my hands in my lap, the sensible words of Solomon ringing in my ears, and considered if there was any way of escaping the fate of the simple.

There was no way. It seemed hard that without being exactly of the simple I yet should be doomed to their fate. And outside it was one of those cold windy mornings when male relations insist on taking one for what they call a run—as if one were a dog—in order to go through the bleak process they describe as getting one's cobwebs blown off. I can't bear being parted from my cobwebs. I never want them blown off. Uncle Rudolph is small and active, besides having since my aunt's death considerably dwindled beneath his apron, and I felt sure he intended to run me up the mountain after breakfast, and, having got me breathless and speechless on to some cold rock, sit with me there and say all the things I am dreading having to hear.

It was quite difficult to get myself to go downstairs. I seemed rooted. I knew that, seeing that I am that unfortunately situated person the hostess, my duty lay in morning smiles behind the coffee pot; but the conviction of what was going to happen to me after the coffee pot kept me rooted, even when the bell had rung twice.

When, however, after the second ringing quick footsteps pattered along the passage to my door I did get up,—jumped up, afraid of what might be coming-in. Bedrooms are no real protection from uncles. Those quick footsteps might easily be Uncle Rudolph's. I hurried across to the door and pulled it open, so that at least by coming out I might stop his coming in; and there was Mrs. Antoine, her hand lifted up to knock.

'*Ces dames et Monsieur l'Evêque attendent,*' she said, with an air of reproachful surprise.

'*Il n'est pas un évêque,*' I replied a little irritably, for I knew I was in the wrong staying upstairs like that, and naturally resented not being allowed to be in the wrong in peace. '*Il est seulement presque un.*'

Mrs. Antoine said nothing to that, but stepping aside to let me pass informed me rather severely that the coffee had been on the table a whole quarter of an hour.

'*Comment appelle-t-on chez vous,*' I said, lingering in the doorway to gain time, '*ce qui vient devant un évêque?*'

'*Ce qui vient devant un évêque?*' repeated Mrs. Antoine doubtfully.

'*Oui. L'espèce de monsieur qui n'est pas tout à fait évêque mais presque?*'

Mrs. Antoine knit her brows. '*Ma foi*—' she began.

'*Oh, j'ai oublié,*' I said. '*Vous n'êtes plus catholique. Il n'y a rien comme des évêques et comme les messieurs qui sont presque évêques dans votre église protestante, n'est-ce pas?*'

'*Mais rien, rien, rien,*' asseverated Mrs. Antoine vehemently, her hands spread out, her shoulders up to her ears, passionately protesting the empty purity of her adopted church,—'*mais rien du tout, du tout. Madame peut venir un dimanche voir....*'

Then, having cleared off these imputations, she switched back to the coffee. '*Le café—Madame désire que j'en fasse encore? Ces dames et Monsieur l'Evêque—*'

'*Il n'est pas un év—*'

'Ah—here you are!' exclaimed my uncle, his head appearing at the top of the stairs. 'I was just coming to see if there was anything the matter. Here she is—coming, coming!' he called out genially to the others; and on my hurrying to join him, for I am not one to struggle against the inevitable, he put his arm through mine and we went down together.

Having got me to the bottom he placed both hands on my shoulders and twisted me round to the light. 'Dear child,' he said, scrutinizing my face while he held me firmly in this position, 'we were getting quite anxious about you. Mrs. Barnes feared you might be ill, and was already contemplating remedies—' I shuddered—'however—' he twisted me round to Mrs. Barnes—'nothing ill about this little lady, Mrs. Barnes, eh?'

Then he took my chin between his finger and thumb and kissed me lightly, gaily even, on each cheek, and then, letting me go, he rubbed his hands and briskly approached the table, all the warm things on which were swathed as usual when I am late either in napkins or in portions of Mrs. Barnes's clothing.

'Come along—come along, now,—breakfast, breakfast,' cried my uncle. '*For these and all Thy mercies Lord*—' he continued with hardly a break, his eyes shut, his hands outspread over Mrs. Barnes's white woollen shawl in benediction.

We were overwhelmed. The male had arrived and taken us in hand. But we were happily overwhelmed, judging from Mrs. Barnes's face. For the first time since she has been with me the blessing of heaven had been implored and presumably obtained for her egg, and I realised from her expression as she ate it how much she had felt the daily enforced consumption, owing to my graceless habits, of eggs unsanctified. And Dolly too looked pleased, as she always does when her poor Kitty is happy. I alone wasn't. Behind the coffee pot I sat pensive. I knew too well what was before me. I distrusted my uncle's gaiety. He had thought it all out in the night, and had decided that the best line of approach to the painful subject he had come to discuss would be one of cheerful affection. Certainly I had never seen him in such spirits; but then I haven't seen him since my aunt's death.

'Dear child,' he said, when the table had been picked up and carried off bodily by the Antoines from our midst, leaving us sitting round nothing with the surprised feeling of sudden nakedness that, as I have already explained, this way of clearing away produces—my uncle was actually surprised for a moment into silence,—'dear child, I would like to take you for a little run before lunch.'

'Yes, Uncle Rudolph?'

'That we may get rid of our cobwebs.'

'Yes, Uncle Rudolph.'

'I know you are a quick-limbed little lady—'

'Yes, Uncle Rudolph?'

'So you shall take the edge off my appetite for exercise.'

'Yes, Uncle Rudolph.'

'Then perhaps this afternoon one or other of these ladies—' I noted his caution in not suggesting both.

'Oh, delightful,' Mrs. Barnes hastened to assure him. 'We shall be only too pleased to accompany you. We are great walkers. We think a very great deal of the benefits to be derived from regular exercise. Our father brought us up to a keen appreciation of its necessity. If it were not that we so strongly feel that the greater part of each day should be employed in some useful pursuit, we would spend it, I believe, almost altogether in outdoor exercise.'

'Why not go with my uncle this morning, then?' I asked, catching at a straw. 'I've got to order dinner—'

'Oh no, no—not on *any* account. The Dean's wishes—'

But who should pass through the hall at that moment, making for the small room where I settle my household affairs, his arms full of the monthly books, but Antoine. It is the first of October. Pay day. I had forgotten. And for this one morning, at least, I knew that I was saved.

'Look,' I said to Mrs. Barnes, nodding in the direction of Antoine and his burden.

I felt certain she would have all the appreciation of the solemnity, the undeferability, of settling up that is characteristic of the virtuous poor; she would understand that even the wishes of deans must come second to this holy household rite.

'Oh, how unfortunate!' she exclaimed. 'Just this day of all days—your uncle's first day.'

But there was nothing to be done. She saw that. And besides, never was a woman so obstinately determined as I was to do my duty.

'Dear Uncle Rudolph,' I said very amiably—I did suddenly feel very amiable—'I'm so sorry. This is the one day in the month when I am tethered. *Any* other day—'

And I withdrew with every appearance of reluctant but indomitable virtue into my little room and stayed there shut in safe till I heard them go out.

64

From the window I could see them presently starting off up the mountain, actively led by my uncle who hadn't succeeded in taking only one, Mrs. Barnes following with the devoutness—she who in our walks goes always first and chooses the way—of an obedient hen, and some way behind, as though she disliked having to shed her cobwebs as much as I do, straggled Dolly. Then, when they had dwindled into just black specks away up the slope, I turned with lively pleasure to paying the books.

Those blessed books! If only I could have gone on paying them over and over again, paying them all day! But when I had done them, and conversed about the hens and bees and cow with Antoine, and it was getting near lunch-time, and at any moment through the window I might see the three specks that had dwindled appearing as three specks that were swelling, I thought I noticed I had a headache.

Addings-up often give me a headache, especially when they won't, which they curiously often won't, add up the same twice running, so that it was quite likely that I *had* got a headache. I sat waiting to be quite sure, and presently, just as the three tiny specks appeared on the sky line, I was quite sure; and I came up here and put myself to bed. For, I argued, it isn't grape-stones this time, it's sums, and Mrs. Barnes can't dose me for what is only arithmetic; also, even if Uncle Rudolph insists on coming to my bedside he can't be so inhumane as to torment somebody who isn't very well.

So here I have been ever since snugly in bed, and I must say my guests have been most considerate. They have left me almost altogether alone. Mrs. Barnes did look in once, and when I said, closing my eyes, 'It's those tradesmens' books—' she understood immediately, and simply nodded her head and disappeared.

Dolly came and sat with me for a little, but we hadn't said much before Mrs. Antoine brought a message from my uncle asking her to go down to tea.

'What are you all doing?' I asked.

'Oh, just sitting round the fire not talking,' she said, smiling.

'*Not* talking?' I said, surprised.

But she was gone.

Perhaps, I thought, they're not talking for fear of disturbing me. This really was most considerate.

As for Uncle Rudolph, he hasn't even tried to come and see me. The only sign of life he has made was to send me the current number of the *Nineteenth Century* he brought out with him, in which he has an article,—a very good one. Else he too has been quite quiet; and I have read, and I have pondered, and I have written this, and now it really is bedtime and I'm going to sleep.

Well, a whole day has been gained anyhow, and I have had hours and hours of complete peace. Rather a surprising lot of peace, really. It *is* rather surprising, I think. I mean, that they haven't wanted to come and see me more. Nobody has even been to say goodnight to me. I think I like being said goodnight to. Especially if nobody does say it.

October 2nd.

Twenty-four hours sometimes produce remarkable changes. These have.

Again it is night, and again I'm in my room on my way to going to sleep; but before I get any sleepier I'll write what I can about to-day, because it has been an extremely interesting day. I knew that what we wanted was a man.

At breakfast, to which I proceeded punctually, refreshed by my retreat yesterday, armed from head to foot in all the considerations I had collected during those quiet hours most likely to make me immune from Uncle Rudolph's inevitable attacks, having said my prayers and emptied my mind of weakening memories, I found my three guests silent. Uncle Rudolph's talkativeness, so conspicuous at yesterday's breakfast, was confined at to-day's to saying grace. Except for that, he didn't talk at all. And neither, once having said her Amen, did Mrs. Barnes. Neither did Dolly, but then she never does.

'I've not got a headache,' I gently said at last, looking round at them.

Perhaps they were still going on being considerate, I thought. At least, perhaps Mrs. Barnes was. My uncle's silence was merely ominous of what I was in for, of how strongly, after another night's thinking it out, he felt about my affairs and his own lamentable connection with them owing to God's having given me to him for a niece. But Mrs.

Barnes—why didn't *she* talk? She couldn't surely intend, because once I had a headache, to go on tiptoe for the rest of our days together?

Nobody having taken any notice of my first announcement I presently said, 'I'm very well indeed, thank you, this morning.'

At this Dolly laughed, and her eyes sent little morning kisses across to me. She, at least, was in her normal state.

'Aren't you—' I looked at the other two unresponsive breakfasting heads—'aren't you glad?'

'Very,' said Mrs. Barnes. 'Very.' But she didn't raise her eyes from her egg, and my uncle again took no notice.

So then I thought I might as well not take any notice either, and I ate my breakfast in dignity and retirement, occasionally fortifying myself against what awaited me after it by looking at Dolly's restful and refreshing face.

Such an unclouded face; so sweet, so clean, so sunny with morning graciousness. Really an ideal breakfast-table face. Fortunate Juchs and Siegfried, I thought, to have had it to look forward to every morning. That they were undeserving of their good fortune I patriotically felt sure, as I sat considering the gentle sweep of her eyelashes while she buttered her toast. Yet they did, both of them, make her happy; or perhaps it was that she made them happy, and caught her own happiness back again, as it were on the rebound. With any ordinarily kind and decent husband this must be possible. That she *had* been happy was evident, for unhappiness leaves traces, and I've never seen an object quite so unmarked, quite so candid as Dolly's intelligent and charming brow.

We finished our breakfast in silence; and no sooner had the table been plucked out from our midst by the swift, disconcerting Antoines, than my uncle got up and went to the window.

There he stood with his back to us.

'Do you feel equal to a walk?' he asked, not turning round.

Profound silence.

We three, still sitting round the blank the vanished table had left, looked at each other, our eyes inquiring mutely, 'Is it I?'

But I knew it was me.

'Do you mean me, Uncle Rudolph?' I therefore asked; for after all it had best be got over quickly.

'Yes, dear child.'

'Now?'

'If you will.'

'There's no esc—you don't think the weather too horrid?'

'Bracing.'

I sighed, and went away to put on my nailed boots.

Relations ... what right had he ... as though I hadn't suffered horribly ... and on such an unpleasant morning ... if at least it had been fine and warm ... but to be taken up a mountain in a bitter wind so as to be made miserable on the top....

And two hours later, when I was perched exactly as I had feared on a cold rock, reached after breathless toil in a searching wind, perched draughtily and shorn of every cob-web I could ever in my life have possessed, helplessly exposed to the dreaded talking-to, Uncle Rudolph, settling himself at my feet, after a long and terrifying silence during which I tremblingly went over my defences in the vain effort to assure myself that perhaps I wasn't going to be *much* hurt, said:

'How does she spell it?'

Really one is very fatuous. Absorbed in myself, I hadn't thought of Dolly.

October 3rd.

It was so late last night when I got to that, that I went to bed. Now it is before breakfast, and I'll finish about yesterday.

Uncle Rudolph had taken me up the mountain only to talk of Dolly. Incredible as it may seem, he has fallen in love. At first sight. At sixty. I am sure a woman can't do that, so that this by itself convinces me he is a man. Three days ago I wrote in this very book that a dean isn't quite my idea of a man. I retract. He is.

Well, while I was shrinking and shivering on my own account, waiting for him to begin digging about among my raw places, he said instead, 'How does she spell it?' and threw my thoughts into complete confusion.

Blankly I gazed at him while I struggled to rearrange them on this new basis. It was such an entirely unexpected question. I did not at this stage dream of what had happened to him. It never would have occurred to me that Dolly would have so immediate an effect, simply by sitting there, simply by producing her dimple at the right moment. Attractive as she is, it is her ways rather than her looks that are so adorable; and what could Uncle Rudolph have seen of her ways in so brief a time? He has simply fallen in love with a smile. And he sixty. And he one's uncle. Amazing Dolly; irresistible apparently, to uncles.

'Do you mean Mrs. Jewks's name?' I asked, when I was able to speak.

'Yes,' said my uncle.

'I haven't seen it written,' I said, restored so far by my relief—for Dolly had saved me—that I had the presence of mind to hedge. I was obliged to hedge. In my mind's eye I saw Mrs. Barnes's face imploring me.

'No doubt,' said my uncle after another silence, 'it is spelt on the same principle as Molyneux.'

'Very likely,' I agreed.

'It sounds as though her late husband's family might originally have been French.'

'It does rather.'

'Possibly Huguenot.'

'Yes.'

'I was much astonished that she should be a widow.'

'*Yet not one widow but two widows....*' ran at this like a refrain in my mind, perhaps because I was sitting so close to a dean. Aloud I said, for by now I had completely recovered, 'Why, Uncle Rudolph? Widows do abound.'

'Alas, yes. But there is something peculiarly virginal about Mrs. Jewks.'

I admitted that this was so. Part of Dolly's attractiveness is the odd impression she gives of untouchedness, of gay aloofness.

My uncle broke off a stalk of the withered last summer's grass and began nibbling it. He was lying on his side a little below me, resting on his elbow. His black, neat legs looked quaint stuck through the long yellow grass. He had taken off his hat, hardy creature, and the wind blew his grey hair this way and that, and sometimes flattened it down in a fringe over his eyes. When this happened he didn't look a bit like anybody good, but he pushed it back each time, smoothing it down again with an abstracted carefulness, his eyes fixed on the valley far below. He wasn't seeing the valley.

'How long has the poor young thing—' he began.

'You will be surprised to hear,' I interrupted him, 'that Mrs. Jewks is forty.'

'Really,' said my uncle, staring round at me. 'Really. That is indeed surprising.' And after a pause he added, 'Surprising and gratifying.'

'Why gratifying, Uncle Rudolph?' I inquired.

'When did she lose her husband?' he asked, taking no notice of my inquiry.

The preliminary to an accurate answer to this question was, of course, Which? But again a vision of Mrs. Barnes's imploring face rose before me, and accordingly, restricting myself to Juchs, I said she had lost him shortly before the war.

'Ah. So he was prevented, poor fellow, from having the honour of dying for England.'

'Yes, Uncle Rudolph.'

'Poor fellow. Poor fellow.'

'Yes.'

'Poor fellow. Well, he was spared knowing what he had missed. At least he was spared that. And she—his poor wife—how did she take it?'

'Well, I think.'

'Yes. I can believe it. She wouldn't—I am very sure she wouldn't—intrude her sorrows selfishly on others.'

It was at this point that I became aware my uncle had fallen in love. Up to this, oddly enough, it hadn't dawned on me. Now it did more than dawned, it blazed.

I looked at him with a new and startled interest. 'Uncle Rudolph,' I said impetuously, no longer a distrustful niece talking to an uncle she suspects, but an equal with an equal, a human being with another human being, 'haven't you ever thought of marrying again? It's quite a long time now since Aunt Winifred—'

'Thought?' said my uncle, his voice sounding for the first time simply, ordinarily human, without a trace in it of the fatal pulpit flavour, 'Thought? I'm always thinking of it.'

And except for his apron and gaiters he might have been any ordinary solitary little man eating out his heart for a mate.

'But then why don't you? Surely a deanery of all places wants a wife in it?'

'Of course it does. Those strings or rooms empty, echoing. It shouts for a wife. Shouts, I tell you. At least mine does. But I've never found—I hadn't seen—'

He broke off, biting at the stalk of grass.

'But I remember you,' I went on eagerly, 'always surrounded by flocks of devoted women. Weren't any of them—?'

'No,' said my uncle shortly. And after a second of silence he said again, and so loud that I jumped, 'No!' And then he went on even more violently, 'They didn't give me a chance. They never let me alone a minute. After Winifred's death they were like flies. Stuck to me—made me sick—great flies crawling—' And he shuddered, and shook himself as though he were shaking off the lot of them.

I looked at him in amazement. 'Why,' I cried, 'you're talking exactly like a man!'

But he, staring at the view without seeing an inch of it, took no heed of me, and I heard him say under his breath as though I hadn't been there at all, 'My God, I'm so lonely at night!'

That finished it. In that moment I began to love my uncle. At this authentic cry of forlornness I had great difficulty in not bending over and putting my arms round him,—just to comfort him, just to keep him warm. It must be a dreadful thing to be sixty and all alone. You look so grown up. You look as though you must have so many resources, so few needs; and you are accepted as provided for, what with your career accomplished, and your houses and servants and friends and books and all the rest of it—all the empty, meaningless rest of it; for really you are the most miserable of motherless cold babies, conscious that you are motherless, conscious that nobody soft and kind and adoring is ever again coming to croon over you and kiss you good-night and be there next morning to smile when you wake up.

'Uncle Rudolph—' I began.

Then I stopped, and bending over took the stalk of grass he kept on biting out of his hand.

'I can't let you eat any more of that,' I said. 'It's not good for you.'

And having got hold of his hand I kept it.

There now, I said, holding it tight.

He looked up at me vaguely, absorbed in his thoughts; then, realising how tight his hand was being held, he smiled.

'You dear child,' he said, scanning my face as though he had never seen it before.

'Yes?' I said, smiling in my turn and not letting go of his hand. 'I like that. I didn't like any of the other dear children I was.'

'Which other dear children?'

'Uncle Rudolph,' I said, 'let's go home. This is a bleak place. Why do we sit here shivering forlornly when there's all that waiting for us down there?'

And loosing his hand I got on to my feet, and when I was on them I held out both my hands to him and pulled him up, and he standing lower than where I was our eyes were then on a level.

'All what?' he asked, his eyes searching mine.

'Oh, Uncle Rudolph! Warmth and Dolly, of course.'

October 4th.

But it hasn't been quite so simple. Nothing last night was different. My uncle remained tongue-tied. Dolly sat waiting to smile at anecdotes that he never told. Mrs. Barnes knitted uneasily, already fearing, perhaps, because of his strange silence, that he somehow may have scented Siegfried, else how inexplicable his silence after that one bright, wonderful first evening and morning.

It was I last night who did the talking, it was I who took up the line, abandoned by my uncle, of wholesome entertainment. I too told anecdotes; and when I had told all the ones I knew and still nobody said anything, I began to tell all the ones I didn't know. Anything rather than that continued uncomfortable silence. But how very difficult it was. I grew quite damp with effort. And nobody except Dolly so much as smiled; and even Dolly, though she smiled, especially when I embarked on my second series of anecdotes, looked at me with a mild inquiry, as if she were wondering what was the matter with me.

Wretched, indeed, is the hostess upon whose guests has fallen, from whatever cause, a blight.

October 5th.

Crabbe's son, in the life he wrote of his father, asks: '*Will it seem wonderful when we consider how he was situated at this time, that with a most affectionate heart, a peculiar attachment to female society, and with unwasted passions, Mr. Crabbe, though in his sixty-second year should have again thought of marriage? I feel satisfied that no one will be seriously shocked with such an evidence of the freshness of his feelings.*'

A little shocked; Crabbe's son was prepared to allow this much; but not *seriously.*

Well, it is a good thing my uncle didn't live at that period, for it would have gone hard with him. His feelings are more than fresh, they are violent.

October 6th.

While Dolly is in the room Uncle Rudolph never moves, but sits tongue-tied staring at her. If she goes away he at once gets up and takes me by the arm and walks me off on to the terrace, where in a biting wind we pace up and down.

Our positions are completely reversed. It is I now who am the wise old relative, counselling, encouraging, listening to outpours. Up and down we pace, up and down, very fast because of the freshness of Uncle's Rudolph's feelings and also of the wind, arm in arm, I trying to keep step, he not bothering about such things as step, absorbed in his condition, his hopes, his fears—especially his fears. For he is terrified lest, having at last found the perfect woman, she won't have him. 'Why should she?' he asks almost angrily, 'Why should she? Tell me why she should.'

'I can't tell you,' I say, for Uncle Rudolph and I are now the frankest friends. 'But I can't tell you either why she shouldn't. Think how nice you are, Uncle Rudolph. And Dolly is naturally very affectionate.'

'She is perfect, perfect,' vehemently declares my uncle.

And Mrs. Barnes, who from the window watches us while we walk, looks with anxious questioning eyes at my face when we come in. What can my uncle have to talk about so eagerly to me when he is out on the terrace, and why does he stare in such stony silence at Dolly when he comes in? Poor Mrs. Barnes.

October 7th.

The difficulty about Dolly for courting purposes is that she is never to be got alone, not even into a corner out of earshot of Mrs. Barnes. Mrs. Barnes doesn't go away for a moment, except together with Dolly. Wonderful how clever she is at it. She is obsessed by terror lest the horrid marriage to the German uncle should somehow be discovered. If she was afraid of my knowing it she is a hundred times more afraid of Uncle Rudolph's knowing it. So persistent is her humility, so great and remote a dignitary does he seem to her, that the real situation hasn't even glimmered on her. All she craves is to keep this holy and distinguished man's good opinion, to protect her Dolly, her darling erring one, from his just but unbearable contempt. Therefore she doesn't budge. Dolly is never to be got alone.

'A man,' said my uncle violently to me this morning, 'can't propose to a woman before her sister.'

'You've quite decided you're going to?' I asked, keeping up with him as best I could, trotting beside him up and down the terrace.

'The minute I can catch her alone. I can't stand any more of this. I must know. If she won't have me—my God, if she won't have me—!'

I laid hold affectionately of his arm. 'Oh, but she will,' I said reassuringly. 'Dolly is rather a creature of habit, you know.'

'You mean she has got used to marriage—'

'Well, I do think she is rather used to it. Uncle Rudolph,' I went on, hesitating as I have hesitated a dozen times these last few days as to whether I oughtn't to tell him about Juchs—Siegfried would be a shock, but Juchs would be crushing unless very carefully explained—'you don't feel you don't think you'd like to know something more about Dolly first? I mean before you propose?'

'No!' shouted my uncle.

Afterwards he said more quietly that he could see through a brick wall as well as most men, and that Dolly wasn't a brick wall but the perfect woman. What could be told him that he didn't see for himself? Nothing, said my uncle.

What can be done with a man in love? Nothing, say I.

October 8th.

Sometimes I feel very angry with Dolly that she should have got herself so tiresomely mixed up with Germans. How simple everything would be now if only she hadn't! But when I am calm again I realise that she couldn't help it. It is as natural to her to get mixed up as to breathe. Very sweet, affectionate natures are always getting mixed up. I suppose if it weren't for Mrs. Barnes's constant watchfulness and her own earnest desire never again to distress poor Kitty, she would at an early stage of their war wanderings have become some ardent Swiss hotelkeeper's wife. Just to please him; just because else he would be miserable. Dolly ought to be married. It is the only certain way of saving her from marriage.

October 9th.

It is snowing. The wind howls, and the snow whirls, and we can't go out and so get away from each other. Uncle Rudolph is obliged, when Dolly isn't there, to continue sitting with Mrs. Barnes. He can't to-day hurry me out on to the terrace. There's only the hall in this house to sit in, for that place I pay the household books in is no more than a cupboard.

Uncle Rudolph could just bear Mrs. Barnes when he could get away from her; to-day he can't bear her at all. Everything that should be characteristic of a dean—patience, courtesy, kindliness, has been stripped off him by his eagerness to propose and the impossibility of doing it. There's nothing at all left now of what he was but that empty symbol, his apron.

October 10th.

My uncle is fermenting with checked, prevented courting. And he ought to be back in England. He ought to have gone back almost at once, he says. He only came out for three or four days—

'Yes; just time to settle *me* in,' I said.

'Yes,' he said, smiling, 'and then take you home with me by the ear.'

He has some very important meetings he is to preside at coming off soon, and here he is, hung up. It is Mrs. Barnes who is the cause of it, and naturally he isn't very nice to her. In vain does she try to please him; the one thing he wants her to do, to go away and leave him with Dolly, she of course doesn't. She sits there, saying meek things about the weather, expressing a modest optimism, ready to relinquish even that if my uncle differs, becoming, when he takes up a book, respectfully quiet, ready the moment he puts it down to rejoice with him if he wishes to rejoice or weep with him if he prefers weeping; and the more she is concerned to give satisfaction the less well-disposed is he towards her. He can't forgive her inexplicable fixedness. Her persistent, unintermittent gregariousness is incomprehensible to him. All he wants, being reduced to simplicity by love, is to be left alone with Dolly. He can't understand, being a man, why if he wants this he shouldn't get it.

'You're not kind to Mrs. Barnes,' I said to him this afternoon. 'You've made her quite unnatural. She is cowed.'

'I am unable to like her,' said my uncle shortly.

'You are quite wrong not to. She has had bitter troubles, and is all goodness. I don't think I ever met anybody so completely unselfish.'

70

'I wish she would go and be unselfish in her own room, then,' said my uncle.

'I don't know you,' I said, shrugging my shoulders. 'You arrived here dripping unction and charitableness, and now—'

'Why doesn't she give me a chance?' he cried. 'She never budges. These women who stick, who can't bear to be by themselves—good heavens, hasn't she prayers she ought to be saying, and underclothes she ought to mend?'

'I don't believe you care so very much for Dolly after all,' I said, 'or you would be kind to the sister she is so deeply devoted to.'

This sobered him. 'I'll try,' said my uncle; and it was quite hard not to laugh at the change in our positions—I the grey-beard now, the wise rebuker, he the hot-headed yet well-intentioned young relative.

October 11th.

I think guests ought to like each other; love each other if they prefer it, but at least like. They too have their duties, and one of them is to resist nourishing aversions; or, if owing to their implacable dispositions they can't help nourishing them, oughtn't they to try very hard not to show it? They should consider the helpless position of the hostess, she who, at any rate theoretically, is bound to be equally attached to them all.

Before my uncle came it is true we had begun to fester, but we festered nicely. Mrs. Barnes and I did it with every mark of consideration and politeness. We were ladies. Uncle Rudolph is no lady; and this little house, which I daresay looks a picture of peace from outside with the snow falling on its roof and the firelight shining in its windows, seethes with elemental passions. Fear, love, anger—they all dwell in it now, all brought into it by him, all coming out of the mixture, so innocuous one would think, so likely, one would think, to produce only the fruits of the spirit,—the mixture of two widows and one clergyman. Wonderful how much can be accomplished with small means. Also, most wonderful the centuries that seem to separate me from those July days when I lay innocently on the grass watching the clouds pass over the blue of the delphinium tops, before ever I had set eyes on Mrs. Barnes and Dolly, and while Uncle Rudolph, far away at home and not even beginning to think of a passport, was being normal in his Deanery.

He has, I am sure, done what he promised and tried to be kinder to Mrs. Barnes, and I can only conclude he was not able to manage it, for I see no difference. He glowers and glowers, and she immovably knits. And in spite of the silence that reigns except when, for a desperate moment, I make an effort to be amusing, there is a curious feeling that we are really living in a state of muffled uproar, in a constant condition of barely suppressed brawl. I feel as though the least thing, the least touch, even somebody coughing, and the house will blow up. I catch myself walking carefully across the hall so as not to shake it, not to knock against the furniture. How secure, how peaceful, of what a great and splendid simplicity do those July days, those pre-guest days, seem now!

October 12th.

I went into Dolly's bedroom last night, crept in on tiptoe because there is a door leading from it into Mrs. Barnes's room, caught hold firmly of her wrist, and led her, without saying a word and taking infinite care to move quietly, into my bedroom. Then, having shut her in, I said, 'What are you going to do about it?'

She didn't pretend not to understand. The candour of Dolly's brow is an exact reflection of the candour of her mind.

'About your uncle,' she said, nodding. 'I like him very much.'

'Enough to marry him?'

'Oh quite. I always like people enough to marry them.' And she added, as though in explanation of this perhaps rather excessively amiable tendency, 'Husbands are so kind.'

'You ought to know,' I conceded.

'I do,' said Dolly, with the sweetest reminiscent smile.

'Uncle Rudolph is only waiting to get you alone to propose,' I said.

Dolly nodded. There was nothing I could tell her that she wasn't already aware of.

'As you appear to have noticed everything,' I said, 'I suppose you have also noticed that he is very much in love with you.'

'Oh yes,' said Dolly placidly.

71

'So much in love that he doesn't seem even to remember that he's a dignitary of the Church, and when he's alone with me he behaves in a way I'm sure the Church wouldn't like at all. Why, he almost swears.'

'*Isn't* it a good thing?' said Dolly, approvingly.

'Yes. But now what is to be done about Siegfried—'

'Dear Siegfried,' murmured Dolly.

'And Juchs—'

'Poor darling,' murmured Dolly.

'Yes, yes. But oughtn't Uncle Rudolph to be told?'

'Of course,' said Dolly, her eyes a little surprised that I should want to know anything so obvious.

'You told me it would kill Kitty if I knew about Juchs. It will kill her twice as much if Uncle Rudolph knows.'

'Kitty won't know anything about it. At least, not till it's all over. My dear, when it comes to marrying I can't be stuck all about with secrets.'

'Do you mean to tell my uncle yourself?'

'Of course,' said Dolly, again with surprise in her eyes.

'When?'

'When he asks me to marry him. Till he does I don't quite see what it has to do with him.'

'And you're not afraid—you don't think your second marriage will be a great shock to him? He being a dean, and nourished on Tables of Affinity?'

'I can't help it if it is. He has got to know. If he loves me enough it won't matter to him, and if he doesn't love me enough it won't matter to him either.'

'Because then his objections to Juchs would be greater than his wish to marry you?'

'Yes,' said Dolly, smiling. 'It would mean,' she went on, 'that he wasn't fond of me *enough*.'

'And you wouldn't mind?'

Her eyes widened a little. 'Why should I mind?'

'No. I suppose you wouldn't, as you're not in love.'

I then remarked that, though I could understand her not being in love with a man my uncle's age, it was my belief that she had never in her life been in love. Not even with Siegfried. Not with anybody.

Dolly said she hadn't, and that she liked people much too much to want to grab at them.

'Grab at them!'

'That's what your being in love does,' said Dolly. 'It grabs.'

'But you've been grabbed yourself, and you liked it. Uncle Rudolph is certainly bent on grabbing you.'

'Yes. But the man gets over it quicker. He grabs and has done with it, and then settles down to the real things,—affection and kindness. A woman hasn't ever done with it. She can't let go. And the poor thing, because she what you call loves, is so dreadfully vulnerable, and gets so hurt, so hurt—'

Dolly began kissing me and stroking my hair.

'I think though,' I said, while she was doing this, 'I'd rather have loved thoroughly— you can call it grabbing if you like, I don't care what ugly words you use—and been vulnerable and got hurt, than never once have felt—than just be a sort of amiable amoeba—'

'Has it occurred to you,' interrupted Dolly, continuing to kiss me—her cheek was against mine, and she was stroking my hair very tenderly—'that if I marry that dear little uncle of yours I shall be your aunt?'

October 13th.

Well, then, if Dolly is ready to marry my uncle and my uncle is dying to marry Dolly, all that remains to be done is to remove Mrs. Barnes for an hour from the hall. An hour would be long enough, I think, to include everything,—five minutes for the proposal, fifteen for presenting Siegfried, thirty-five for explaining Juchs, and five for the final happy mutual acceptances.

This very morning I must somehow manage to get Mrs. Barnes away. How it is to be done I can't think; especially for so long as an hour. Yet Juchs and Siegfried couldn't be rendered intelligible, I feel, in less than fifty minutes between them. Yes; it will have to be an hour.

I have tried over and over again the last few days to lure Mrs. Barnes out of the hall, but it has been useless. Is it possible that I shall have to do something unpleasant to myself, hurt myself, hurt something that takes time to bandage? The idea is repugnant to me; still, things can't go on like this.

I asked Dolly last night if I hadn't better draw Mrs. Barnes's attention to my uncle's lovelorn condition, for obviously the marriage would be a solution of all her difficulties and could give her nothing but extraordinary relief and joy; but Dolly wouldn't let me. She said that it would only agonise poor Kitty to become aware that my uncle was in love, for she would be quite certain that the moment he heard about Juchs horror would take the place of love. How could a dean of the Church of England, Kitty would say, bring himself to take as wife one who had previously been married to an item in the forbidden list of the Tables of Affinity? And Juchs being German would only, she would feel, make it so much more awful. Besides, said Dolly, smiling and shaking her head, my uncle mightn't propose at all. He might change again. I myself had been astonished, she reminded me, at the sudden violent change he had already undergone from unction to very nearly swearing; he might easily under-go another back again, and then what a pity to have disturbed the small amount of peace of mind poor Kitty had.

'She hasn't any, ever,' I said; impatiently, I'm afraid.

'Not very much,' admitted Dolly with wistful penitence. 'And it has all been my fault.'

But what I was thinking was that Kitty never has any peace of mind because she hasn't any mind to have peace in.

I didn't say this, however.

I practised tact.

Later.

Well, it has come off. Mrs. Barnes is out of the hall, and at this very moment Uncle Rudolph and Dolly are alone together in it, proposing and being proposed to. He is telling her that he worships her, and in reply she is gently drawing his attention to Siegfried and Juchs. How much will he mind them? Will he mind them at all? Will his love triumphantly consume them, or, having swallowed Siegfried, will he find himself unable to manage Juchs?

Oh, I love people to be happy! I love them to love each other! I do hope it will be all right! Dolly may say what she likes, but love is the only thing in the world that works miracles. Look at Uncle Rudolph. I'm more doubtful, though, of the result than I would have been yesterday, because what brought about Mrs. Barnes's absence from the hall has made me nervous as to how he will face the disclosing of Juchs.

While I'm waiting I may as well write it down,—by my clock I count up that Dolly must be a third of the way through Siegfried now, so that I've still got three quarters of an hour.

This is what happened:

The morning started badly, indeed terribly. Dolly, bored by being stared at in silence, said something about more wool and went upstairs quite soon after breakfast. My uncle, casting a despairing glance at the window past which the snow was driving, scowled for a moment or two at Mrs. Barnes, then picked up a stale *Times* and hid himself behind it.

To make up for his really dreadful scowl at Mrs. Barnes I began a pleasant conversation with her, but at once she checked me, saying, 'Sh—sh—,' and deferentially indicating, with her knitting needle, my reading uncle.

Incensed by such slavishness, I was about to rebel and insist on talking when he, stirred apparently by something of a bloodthirsty nature that he saw in the *Times*, exclaimed in a very loud voice, 'Search as I may—and I have searched most diligently—I can't find a single good word to say for Germans.'

It fell like a bomb. He hasn't mentioned Germans once. I had come to feel quite safe. The shock of it left me dumb. Mrs. Barnes's knitting needles stopped as if struck. I didn't dare look at her. Dead silence.

My uncle lowered the paper and glanced round at us, expecting agreement, impatient of our not instantly saying we thought as he did.

'Can *you*?' he asked me, as I said nothing, being petrified.

I was just able to shake my head.

'Can *you*?' he asked, turning to Mrs. Barnes.

Her surprising answer—surprising, naturally, to my uncle—was to get up quickly, drop all her wool on the floor, and hurry upstairs.

He watched her departure with amazement. Still with amazement, when she had disappeared, his eyes sought mine.

Why, he said, staring at me aghast, 'why—the woman's a pro-German!'

In my turn I stared aghast.

'Mrs. *Barnes*?' I exclaimed, stung to quite a loud exclamation by the grossness of this injustice.

'Yes,' said my uncle, horrified. 'Yes. Didn't you notice her expression? Good heavens—and I who've taken care not to speak to a pro-German for five years, and had hoped, God willing, never to speak to one again, much less—' he banged his fists on the arms of the chair, and the *Times* slid on to the floor—'much less be under the same roof with one.'

'Well then, you see, God wasn't willing,' I said, greatly shocked.

Here was the ecclesiastic coming up again with a vengeance in all the characteristic anti-Christian qualities; and I was so much stirred by his readiness to believe what he thinks is the very worst of poor, distracted Mrs. Barnes, that I flung caution to the winds and went indignantly on: 'It isn't Mrs. Barnes who is pro-German in this house—it's Dolly.'

'What?' cried my uncle.

'Yes,' I repeated, nodding my head at him defiantly, for having said it I was scared, 'it's Dolly.'

'Dolly?' echoed my uncle, grasping the arms of his chair.

'Perhaps pro-German doesn't quite describe it,' I hurried on nervously, 'and yet I don't know—I think it would. Perhaps it's better to say that she is—she is of an unprejudiced international spirit—'

Then I suddenly realised that Mrs. Barnes was gone. Driven away. Not likely to appear again for ages.

I got up quickly. 'Look here, Uncle Rudolph,' I said, making hastily, even as Mrs. Barnes had made, for the stairs, 'you ask Dolly about it yourself. I'll go and tell her to come down. You ask her about being pro-German. She'll tell you. Only—' I ran back to him and lowered my voice—'propose first. She won't tell you unless you've proposed first.'

Then, as he sat clutching the arms of his chair and staring at me, I bent down and whispered, 'Now's your chance, Uncle Rudolph. You've settled poor Mrs. Barnes for a bit. She won't interrupt. I'll send Dolly—goodbye—good luck!'

And hurriedly kissing him I hastened upstairs to Dolly's room.

Because of the door leading out of it into Mrs. Barnes's room I had to be as cautious as I was last night. I did exactly the same things: went in on tiptoe, took hold of her firmly by the wrist, and led her out without a word. Then all I had to do was to point to the stairs, and at the same time make a face—but a kind face, I hope—at her sister's shut door, and the intelligent Dolly did the rest.

She proceeded with a sober dignity pleasant to watch, along the passage in order to be proposed to. Practice in being proposed to has made her perfect. At the top of the stairs she turned and smiled at me,—her dimple was adorable. I waved my hand; she disappeared; and here I am.

Forty minutes of the hour are gone. She must be in the very middle now of Juchs.

Night.

I knew this little house was made for kindness and love. I've always, since first it was built, had the feeling that it was blest. Sure indeed was the instinct that brought me away from England, doggedly dragging myself up the mountain to tumble my burdens down in this place. It invariably conquers. Nobody can resist it. Nobody can go away from here quite as they arrived, unless to start with they were of those blessed ones who wherever they go

74

carry peace with them in their hearts. From the first I have felt that the worried had only got to come here to be smoothed out, and the lonely to be exhilarated, and the unhappy to be comforted, and the old to be made young. Now to this list must be added: and the widowed to be wedded; because all is well with Uncle Rudolph and Dolly, and the house once more is in its normal state of having no one in it who isn't happy.

For I grew happy—completely so for the moment, and I shouldn't be surprised if I had really done now with the other thing—the minute I caught sight of Uncle Rudolph's face when I went downstairs.

Dolly was sitting by the file looking pleased. My uncle was standing on the rug; and when he saw me he came across to me holding out both his hands, and I stopped on the bottom stair, my hands in his, and we looked at each other and laughed,—sheer happiness we laughed for.

Then we kissed each other, I still on the bottom stair and therefore level with him, and then he said, his face full of that sweet affection for the whole world that radiates from persons in his situation, 'And to think that I came here only to scold you!'

'Yes, Uncle Rudolph,' I said. 'To think of it!'

'Well, if I came to scold I've stayed to love,' he said.

'Which,' said I, while we beamed at each other, 'as the Bible says, is far better.'

Then Dolly went upstairs to tell Mrs. Barnes—lovely to be going to strike off somebody's troubles with a single sentence!—and my uncle confessed to me that for the first time a doubt of Dolly had shadowed his idea of her when I left him sitting there while I fetched her—

'Conceive it—conceive it!' he cried, smiting his hands together. 'Conceive letting Germans—*Germans*, if you please—get even for half an instant between her and me!'—but that the minute he saw her coming down the stairs to him such love of her flooded him that he got up and proposed to her before she had so much as reached the bottom. And it was from the stairs, as from a pulpit, that Dolly, supporting herself on the balustrade, expounded Siegfried and Juchs.

She wouldn't come down till she had finished with them. She was, I gathered, ample over Siegfried, but when it came to Juchs she was profuse. Every single aspect of them both that was most likely to make a dean think it impossible to marry her was pointed out and enlarged upon. She wouldn't, she announced, come down a stair further till my uncle was in full possession of all the facts, while at the same time carefully bearing in mind the Table of Affinity.

'And were you terribly surprised and shocked, Uncle Rudolph?' I asked, standing beside him with our backs to the fire in our now familiar attitude of arm in arm.

My uncle is an ugly little man, yet at that moment I could have sworn that he had the face of an angel. He looked at me and smiled. It was the wonderfullest smile.

'I don't know what I was,' he said. 'When she had done I just said, "My Beloved"—and then she came down.'

October 15th.

This is my last night here, and this is the last time I shall write in my old-age book. To-morrow we all go away together, to Bern, where my uncle and Dolly will be married, and then he takes her to England, and Mrs. Barnes and I will also proceed there, discreetly, by another route.

So are the wanderings of Mrs. Barnes and Dolly ended, and Mrs. Barnes will enter into her idea of perfect bliss, which is to live in the very bosom of the Church with a cathedral almost in her back garden. For my uncle, prepared at this moment to love anybody, also loves Mrs. Barnes, and has invited her to make her home with him. At this moment indeed he would invite everybody to make their homes with him, for not only has he invited me but I heard him most cordially pressing those peculiarly immovable Antoines to use his house as their headquarters whenever they happen to be in England.

I think a tendency to invite runs in the family, for I too have been busy inviting. I have invited Mrs. Barnes to stay with me in London till she goes to the Deanery, and she has accepted. Together we shall travel thither, and together we shall dwell there, I am sure, in that unity which is praised by the Psalmist as a good and pleasant thing.

She will stay with me for the weeks during which my uncle wishes to have Dolly all to himself. I think there will be a great many of those weeks, from what I know of Dolly; but being with a happy Mrs. Barnes will be different from being with her as she was here. She is so happy that she consists entirely of unclouded affection. The puckers from her face, and the fears and concealments from her heart, have all gone together. She is as simple and as transparent as a child. She always was transparent, but without knowing it; now she herself has pulled off her veils, and cordially requests one to look her through and through and see for oneself how there is nothing there but contentment. A little happiness,—what wonders it works! Was there ever anything like it?

This is a place of blessing. When I came up my mountain three months ago, alone and so miserable, no vision was vouchsafed me that I would go down it again one of four people, each of whom would leave the little house full of renewed life, of restored hope, of wholesome looking-forward, clarified, set on their feet, made useful once more to themselves and the world. After all, we're none of us going to be wasted. Whatever there is of good in any of us isn't after all going to be destroyed by circumstances and thrown aside as useless. When I am so foolish—*if* I am so foolish I should say, for I feel completely cured! as to begin thinking backwards again with anything but a benevolent calm, I shall instantly come out here and invite the most wretched of my friends to join me, and watch them and myself being made whole.

The house, I think, ought to be rechristened.

It ought to be called *Chalet du Fleuve Jordan*.

But perhaps my guests mightn't like that.

Lightning Source UK Ltd.
Milton Keynes UK
UKHW022315010621
384752UK00006B/86